NOTHING
BUT
BLACKENED
TEETH

NOTHING
BUT
BLACKENED
TEETH

CASSANDRA KHAW

NIGHTFIRE

A TOM DOHERTY ASSOCIATES BOOK
NEW YORK

NOTHING BUT BLACKENED TEETH

Copyright © 2021 by Zoe Khaw Joo Ee

A Nightfire Book
Published by Tom Doherty Associates
120 Broadway
New York, NY 10271

www.tornightfire.com

Nightfire™ is a trademark of Macmillan Publishing Group, LLC.

The Library of Congress Cataloging-in-Publication Data is available upon request.

ISBN 978-1-250-75941-2 (hardcover)
ISBN 978-1-250-75942-9 (ebook)

Our books may be purchased in bulk for promotional, educational, or business use. Please contact your local bookseller or the Macmillan Corporate and Premium Sales Department at 1-800-221-7945, extension 5442, or by email at MacmillanSpecialMarkets@macmillan.com.

First Edition: October 2021

Printed in the United States of America

10 9 8 7 6 5 4 3 2 1

To my real-life Mouse,
We got out.

NOTHING
BUT
BLACKENED
TEETH

CHAPTER 1

How the fuck are you this rich?" I took in the old vestibule, the wood ceiling that domed our heads. Time etched itself into the shape and stretch of the Heian mansion, its presence apparent in even the texture of the crumbling dark. It felt profane to see the place like this: without curators to chaperone us, no one to say *do not touch* and *be careful, this was old before the word for such things existed.*

That Phillip could finance its desecration—lock, stock, no question—and do so without self-reproach was symptomatic of our fundamental differences. He shrugged, smile cocked like the sure thing that was his whole life.

"I'm— Come on, it's a wedding gift. They're supposed to be extravagant."

"Extravagant is matching Rolex watches. Extrava-gant"—I slowed down for effect, taking time between each syllable—"is a honeymoon trip to Hawaii. This, on the other hand, is . . . This is beyond absurd, dude. You flew us all to Japan. *First class.* And then rented the fucking imperial palace or—"

"It's not a palace! It's just a mansion. And I didn't rent the building, per se. Just got us permits to spend a few nights here."

"Oh. Like that makes this any less ridiculous."

"Ssh. Stop, stop, stop. Don't finish. I get it, I get it." Phillip dropped his suitcases at the door and palmed the back of his neck, looking sheepish. His varsity jacket, still perfectly fitted to his broad quarterback frame, blazed indigo and yellow where it caught the sun. In the dusk, the letters of his name were gilt and glory and good stitching. Poster-boy perfect: every one craved him like a vice. "Seriously, though. It's no big deal."

"No big deal, he says. Freaking billionaires."

"Caaaaat."

Have you ever cannonballed into a cold lake? The shock of an old memory is kind of like that; every neuron singing a bright hosanna: *here we are. You forgot about us, but we didn't forget about you.*

Only one other person had ever said my name that way.

"Is Lin coming?" I licked the corner of a tooth.

"No comment."

You could just about smell the cream on the lip of Phillip's grin, though. I tried not to cringe, to wince, beset by a zoetrope of sudden emotions. I hadn't spoken to Lin since before I checked myself into the hospital for terminal ennui, exhaustion so acute it couldn't be sanitized with sleep, couldn't be remedied by anything but a twist of rope tugged tight. The doctors kept me for six days and then sent me home, pockets stuffed with pills and appointments and placards advocating the commandments of safer living. I spent six months doing the work, a shut-in committed to the betterment of self, university and my study of Japanese literature, both formal and otherwise, shelved, temporarily.

When I came out, there was a wedding and a world so seamlessly closed up around the space where I stood, you'd think I was never there in the first place.

A door thumped shut and we both jumped, turned like cogs. All my grief rilled somewhere else. I swear, if that moment wasn't magic, wasn't everything that is right and good, nothing else in the world is allowed to call itself beautiful. It was perfect. A Hallmark commercial in freeze-frame: autumn leaves, swirling against a backdrop of beech and white cedar; god rays dripping between the boughs; Faiz and Talia emerging, arms looped together, eyes only for each other, smiling so hard that all I wanted to do was promise them that forever will always, eternally, unchangingly be just like this.

Suenomatsuyama nami mo koenamu.

My head jackknifed up. There it was. The stutter of a girl's voice, sweet despite its coarseness, like a square of fabric worn ragged, like a sound carried on the last ragged breath of a failing record player. A hallucination. It had to be. It needed to be.

"You heard something spooky?" said Phillip.

I strong-armed a smile into place. "Yeah. There's a headless lady in the air right there who says that she killed herself because you never called. You shouldn't ghost people, dude. It's bad manners."

His joviality wicked away, his own expression tripping over old memories. "Hey. Look. If you're still mad about—"

"It's old news." I shook my head. "Old and buried."

"I'm still sorry."

I stiffened. "You said that already."

"I know. But that shit that I did, that wasn't cool. You and me—I should have found a better way of ending things, and—" His hands fluttered up and fell in time with the backbeat of his confession, Phillip's expression cragged with the guilt he'd held for years like

a reliquary. This wasn't the first time we'd had this conversation. This wasn't even the tenth, the thirtieth.

Truth was, I hated that he still felt guilty. It wasn't
charitable but apologies didn't exonerate the sinner, only
compelled graciousness from its recipient. The words,
each time they came, so repetitive that I could tune a
clock to their angst, sawed through me. You can't move
forward when someone keeps dragging you back. I
trapped the tip of my tongue between my teeth, bit
down, and exhaled through the sting.

"Old news," I said.

"I'm still sorry."

"Your punishment, I guess, is dealing with bad puns
forever."

"I'd take it." Phillip made a bassoon noise deep in
his lungs, a kind of laugh, and traded his Timberlands
for the pair of slippers he'd bought at a souvenir shop at
the airport. It'd cost him too much, but the attendant,
her lipstick game sharp as a paper cut, had thrown in
her number, and Phillip always folds for wolves in girl-
skin clothing. "Long as you promise you don't spook
the ghosts."

In another life, I had been brave. Growing up where
we did, back in melting-pot Malaysia, down in the trop-
ics where the mangroves spread dense as myths, you
knew to look for ghosts. Superstition was a compass: it

steered your attention through thin alleys, led your eyes to crosswalks filthy with makeshift shrines, offerings and appeasements scattered by traffic. The five of us spent years in restless pilgrimage, searching for the holy dead in Kuala Lumpur. Every haunted house, every abandoned hospital, every storm drain to have clasped a body like a girl's final prayer, we sieved through them all.

And I was always in the vanguard, torchlight in hand, eager to show the way.

"Things change."

A breeze slouched through the decaying shoji screens: lavender, mildew, sandalwood, and rotting incense. Some of the paper panels were peeling in strips, others gnawed to the still vividly lacquered wood, but the tatami mantling the floors—

There was so much, too much of it everywhere, more than even a Heian noble's house should hold, and all of it was pristine. Store-bought fresh even, when the centuries should have chewed the straw to mulch. The sight of it itched under my skin, like someone'd fed those small, black picnic ants through a vein, somehow; got them to spread out under the thin layer of dermis, got them to start digging.

I shuddered. It was possible that someone'd come in to renovate, maybe someone who'd decided that if

the manor was going to house five idiot foreigners, they
might as well make it a bit more livable. But the interior
didn't smell like it'd had people here, not for a long,
long time, and smelled instead like such old buildings
do: green and damp and dark and hungry, hollow as a
stomach that'd forgotten what it was like to eat.

"Does someone use this as a summer house?"

Phillip shrugged. "Probably? I don't know. My guy
didn't want to talk too much about it."

I shook my head. "Because something about this
place doesn't add up."

"We're probably not the only customers in the 'desti-
nation horror' business," said Phillip, grinning. "Relax."

Faiz whistled, interrupting me. "Yeah, this is the
real deal. My man, Phillip. You're a gentleman and six
quarters."

"Was nothing." Phillip bared a bright fierce grin at
the happy couple. "Just some good old-fashioned luck
and the family money put to great use."

"You don't ever quit about that inheritance, do you?"
said Faiz, smile only as far as the spokes of his cheeks,
eyes flat. He cupped an arm around Talia's waist. "We
know you're rich, Phillip."

"Come on, dude. That wasn't what I was trying to
say." Arms spread, body language open as a house with
no doors. You couldn't hate Phillip for long. But Faiz

was trying. "Besides, my money is your money. Brothers to the end, you know?"

Talia was taller, duskier than Faiz. Part Bengali, part Telugu. Legs like stilts, a smile like a Christmas miracle. And when she laughed, low like a note in a cello's long throat, it was as if she had been the one to teach the world the sound. Talia laid long fingers atop the jut of Phillip's shoulder and bowed her head, precociously regal. "Don't fight. Both of you. Not today."

"Who's fighting?" Faiz had a radio voice, an easy-listening tenor just about south of primetime worthy. Nothing some hard living couldn't fix, some good cigarettes and bad whiskey. He wasn't much of anything except doughier than ever. Not fat—not that there was anything wrong with that—but glutinous almost, soft as good clay. Beauty and her unfinished pottery, half-molded, still slick; the tips of Faiz's hair jutting out at the nape, dewed with sweat.

I felt an immediate guilt at the unkind observation. Faiz was my best friend and he'd done more than his share, talking Talia down from walling me out. She and I made eye contact as the boys bantered, their voices prickling like the hackles of a Doberman, short and stark, animosity panting between the niceness, and Talia's expression congealed with dislike.

I stroked a hand over my arm and tried to keep

a smile on. A muscle in Talia's jaw went rigid as she cracked her face into a similar configuration: her smile tense, mineral, bracketed with impatience.

"I didn't think you were actually going to come. Not after everything you had to say about the two of us." Courtesy velveted her voice. Talia peeled from Faiz and strode across the room, closing the distance between us two inches too much. I could smell her: roses and sweet cardamom.

"You two weren't happy," I said, hands burrowed into my pockets, a slight backward lean to the axis of my spine. "I'm glad that you figured out your differences but at the time, you were at each other's throats—"

Talia had almost three inches on me and levered that to her advantage, looming. "Your insistence that we break up didn't help."

"I didn't insist anything." I heard my voice constrict, the registers narrow so much, every syllable caught and was crushed together into a slurry. "I just thought—"

"You nearly cost me everything," Talia said, still staccato in her rage.

"I had both your best interests at heart."

"Are you sure?" Her expression shaded with pity. I glanced at the boys. "Or were you hoping to get Faiz back?"

We *had* dated—if you could call it that. Eight weeks,

no chemistry, not even a kiss, and had we been older, our confidence less flimsy, less dependent on the perceived temperature of our reputations, we'd have known to end it sooner. Something came out of that, at least: a friendship. Guilt-bruised, gestated in the shambles of a stillborn romance. But a friendship nonetheless.

The light deepened in the house, blued where it broke into the corridors.

"I'm fucking sure of it. And Jesus, I don't want your man," I told her with as much detachment as I could scrounge, not wanting to sell Faiz short. Not after all this. "It's been years since we were together and I don't know what more you want from me. I've apologized. I've tried to make it up to you."

Talia let a corner of her lips wither. "You could have stayed home."

"Yeah, well."

The sentence emptied into a surprised flutter of noises as the two guys—men, *barely*, and by definition rather than practice, their egos still too molten—came tumbling back from the periphery. Phillip had Faiz laughingly mounted on a shoulder, a half fireman carry with the latter's elbow stabbed into the divot of Phillip's collarbone. Faiz, he at first looked like he might have been grinning through the debacle, but the way his skin pulled upward from his teeth: that said different. It was a grimace, bared teeth restrained by a membrane of decorum.

"Put my husband down!" Talia fluted, reaching for her groom-to-be.

"I can handle it." A snarling comeback without an anchor, in fact. Phillip could have kept Faiz suspended forever, but he relented as Talia curved a shoulder against him, arms raised like a supplicant. He set Faiz down and took a languid step back, thumbs hooked through his belt buckles, his grin still easy-as-you-please.

"Jackass," said Faiz, dusting the indignity from himself.

"So tell me about this place, Phillip," said Talia, voice billowing in volume, filling the room, the house and its dark. "Tell me this isn't secretly Matsue Castle. Because I'll *kill* myself if it is. I heard they buried a dancing girl in the walls and the castle shakes if anyone even thinks about dancing near it."

The manor seemed to breathe in, drinking her promise. I could tell we all noticed it, all at once, but instead of hightailing it, we bent our heads like this was a baptism.

"The house might hold you to that," I blurted before I could stop myself, and the sheer wrongness of the statement, the weird puppyish earnestness in its jump from my throat, made me cringe. A long year spent making acquaintances with the demons inside you, each new day a fresh covenant. It does things to you. More specifically, it undoes things inside you. To have to barter for the bravery to go outside, pick up the phone, spend ten minutes assured in the upward trajectory of your recovery: that the appointments are enough, that you can be enough, that one day, this will be enough to make things okay again. All those things change you.

Still, no one looked askance. If anything, the words lit something in their expression, the last light of the day etching their faces in rough shadows. Talia held my gaze, her eyes cold black water.

"Luckily," Phillip, and stretched like a dog, long and lazy, completely unselfconscious. Scratched behind his ear, a smile crooking his lips. "This isn't Matsue Castle."

Faiz patted Talia's arm. "Nah, not even Phillip could rent out a place like that."

Phillip tried on abashment, complete with an honest-to-god aw-shucks toe scuffing, but it didn't work. At this point, he'd been homecoming king, class valedictorian, debate captain, chess wunderkind, every type of impressive a boy could hope to be, king of kings in a palace of princes. Even when they try, guys like him can't do self-effacing.

But they can be good sports.

"This is better." I rolled my luggage up against a pillar, slouched carefully against the wood. Despite everything, I was warming to their enthusiasm, partially because it was so much easier to just go along with it, less lonely too. Media's all about the gospel of the lone wolf, but the truth is we're all just sheep.

"But what is *this* exactly?" said Faiz, ever meticulous when love was a mandrel in his deliberations. His fingers bangled Talia's wrist and his smile creased from worry.

"Well." Phillip gutted the word, unstrung it over twenty seconds. "My guy wouldn't give me a name. He said he didn't want anything on record in case—"

"Could have just told you over the phone," said Faiz.

Phillip tapped the side of a finger to his temple. "Didn't want it to be a 'he said, they said' thing either. He was a stickler for the rules."

"I guess it *is* cultural," said Faiz, full of knowing. His mother was Japanese, small-framed and smileless. "Makes sense."

"We have a permit for this, though. Right?" said Talia, a wobble in her gilded prep-school inflections.

"Yeah. We do. Don't worry about that." Phillip palmed the back of his neck. "Well. Sort of. We have a permit allowing us to access the land here. The mansion's sort of . . . collateral benefit."

"Okay. So, we don't have a name," began Faiz, counting sins on his fingers. "We don't actually have a permit to be here. But we have booze, food, sleeping bags, a youthful compulsion to do stupid shit—"

"And a hunger for a good ghost story," said Talia. The late light did beautiful things to her skin, burnished her in gold. "What is the scoop on this mansion?"

"I don't know," Phillip said, the singsong timbre of his voice familiar, the sound of it like a coyote lying about where he'd left the sun. "But rumour has it that this was once supposed to be the site of a beautiful wedding. Unfortunately, the groom never showed up. He died along the way."

"If you die," said Talia, pinching a curd of Faiz's waist between her fingers, "I'm gonna marry Phillip instead. Just so you know."

Phillip smiled at the proclamation like he'd heard it ten times before from ten thousand other women, knew every syllable was meant, would already be true if it weren't for fraternal bonds, and I was the only one who saw how Faiz's answering smile wouldn't climb to his eyes.

"I don't think you're allowed to marry your priest," Faiz said, easy as anything. "But if you had to get a replacement, I'd rather you pick Cat."

"Ugh," I said. "Not my type."

"I'd rather die an old maid. No offense," said Talia.

"None taken."

"Anyway," said Phillip with a clearing of his throat. "The bride took her abandonment in stride and told her wedding guests to bury her in the foundation of the house."

"Alive?" I whispered. I thought of a girl holding both hands to her mouth, swallowing air and then dirt, her hair and the hems of her wedding dress becoming heavier with every shovel's worth of soil to come down.

"Alive," said Phillip. "She said she had promised to wait for him and she would. She'd keep the house standing until his ghost finally came home."

Silence placed itself to rest along the house and upon our tongues.

"And every year after that, they buried a new girl in the walls," said Phillip.

"Why," started Faiz, startling somehow at this revelation, "the fuck would they do that?"

"Because it gets lonely down in the dirt," Phillip continued, while I held my tongue to the steeple of my mouth. "Why do you think there are so many stories of ghosts trying to get people to kill themselves? Because they miss having someone there, someone warm.

It doesn't matter how many corpses are lying in the soil with them. It's not the same. The dead miss the sun. It's dark down there."

"That's—" Talia walked a hand along Faiz's arm, a gesture that said *look, you have to understand that this belongs to me.* Her eyes found mine, liquid and unkind. In that instant, I wanted badly to tell her again that the past was so sepulchered in poor choices, you couldn't get Faiz and me back together for bourbon enough to brine New Orleans. But that wasn't the point. "—That's pretty fucking metal."

"We'll be fine. Freshly certified man of the cloth right here." Phillip pounded his sternum with a fist, laughing, and Talia immediately kissed Faiz in answer. He took her knuckles to his mouth, grazed each of them with his lips in turn. I stared at the skins of woven straw thatching the floors, shuddered despite myself. I was abruptly dumbstruck by a profound curiosity.

How many dead and dismembered women laid folded in these walls and under these floors, in the rafters that ribbed the ceiling and along those broad steps, barely visible in the murk?

Tradition insists the offerings be buried alive, able to breathe and bargain through the process, their funerary garments debased by shit, piss, and whatever other fluids we extrude on the cusp of death. I couldn't shake the idea of an eminently practical family, one that understood that bone won't rot where wood might, ordering their workers to stack girls like bricks. Arms here, legs there, a vein of skulls wefted into the manor's framing, insurance against a time when traditional architecture might fail. Might as well. They were here for the long haul. One day, these doors would open and wedding guests would pour through and there would be a marriage, come the cataclysm or modern civilization.

The house would wait forever until it happened.

One girl each year. Two hundred and six bones times a thousand years. More than enough calcium to keep this house standing until the stars ate themselves clean, picked the sinew from their own shining bones.

All for one girl as she waited and waited.

Alone in the dirt and the dark.

"Cat?"

I blinked free of my fugue, fingers clenched around my wrist. "I'm okay."

"You sure?" Phillip cocked a worried look, hair haloed by a slant of owl-light. "You don't look like you're fine. Is it—"

"Leave it," Faiz said softly. The joy'd gone out of his expression, replaced by concern, a twitch of protective anger that carried to his teeth, his lips peeling back. I wagged my head, smoothed out a smile. It's fine. Everything's fine. "Cat knows we're here if she needs us."

The look on my face must have been a sight to see because Phillip flinched and ducked out of the room, mumbling about mistakes, cheeks blotching. I ran through my to-do list thrice, counted out chores, precautions, a thousand trivialities, until order restored itself by way of monotony. I glanced over, breathing easy again, to see Faiz and Talia bent together like congregants, a steeple made of their bodies, foreheads touching. It was impossible to miss the cue.

Exit, stage anywhere.

So, I followed the shutter-pop of Phillip's new camera to where he stood in an antechamber, painted by the evening penumbra, dusk colors: gold and pink. A moting of dust spiraled in the damp air, glinting palely where particles caught in the cooling sun. At some point, the roof here had fissured, letting the weather slop through. The flooring underneath was rotten, green where the mould and ferns and whorls of thick moss had taken root in the mulch.

"Sorry."

I shrugged. There were wildflowers by the lungful, swelling at Phillip's feet. "It's fine."

His eyebrows went up.

A bird shrilled its laughter. Through the wound in the roof, I saw a flash of ambergris and tanzanite, the teal of a feathered throat. Phillip stretched, a Rembrandt in high-definition. "Cat—"

"You were just worried about a friend. It happens."

"Yeah, but—"

"I'm not going to throw myself off a building because you were trying to be nice. That's not how it works." I swallowed.

"Okay. Just . . . tell me what you need, all right? I don't—I don't always know the right things to say. I mean, I'm okay at some things, but—"

Like women, I thought. Like being a star, being loved, being hungered for. Phillip excelled at inciting want, particularly the kind that tottered on the border of worship. Small wonder he was so inept at compassion sometimes. Every religion is a one-way relationship.

To our right, a half-opened fusuma—the opaque panel stood floor to ceiling, slid noiselessly on its rail when I pushed—that opened into a garden: a neat square of emerald bracketed by verandahs, an algae-swallowed pool at its heart. The foliage crawled with red higanbana, dead men's flowers.

I ran my fingers through my hair. I was suddenly, irrevocably exhausted, and the thought of having to exorcise Phillip's guilt again, to assure him that he wasn't a bad man, nauseated me. In lieu of comfort, I groped for inanities.

"When did you date Talia? Was it after or while we were seeing each other?"

"Cat?" A laugh startled from him.

"I don't mean that as an accusation. It doesn't matter. I was just wondering." I stroked a finger along the bamboo lattice, came out with dust, decomposing plant material, an oiliness that I couldn't place.

"About a month after. But we weren't exclusive or anything."

"You never did like the exclusive thing, no."

"It's not that." So much sincerity in those gold-blue eyes, crowns of honey around black pupils. "It's just we were kids. We're still kids. These relationships won't last us into adulthood. Most of them won't. Talia and Faiz, that's something else. Anyway. When I'm older, I'll settle down. But these are the best years of my life and I don't want to waste them shackled to a person I won't like at thirty."

His gaze became pleading.

"You understand, right?" said Phillip, yearning for affirmation.

"I'm just wondering if Faiz knows you two were together."

He stilled.

"That's on Talia to tell him. Not me."

I considered my next words.

"In case he doesn't know, I feel like you should make it a point to pretend that you two weren't ever an item."

Guileless, the reply: "Why?"

I thought of Faiz and his teeth, bared and blunt and bitter. "Faiz might not like suddenly finding out that you slept with his fiancée."

"He's an adult. And male. He's not going to care about someone's sexual history."

"Better safe than sorry, Phillip." I paused. "Also, fuck you. Faiz is an adult who can make his own decisions, but you're a kid who shouldn't commit yet?"

"Hey, people mature at different speeds."

"Jesus. Fine. Just make sure you don't let Faiz know you used to sleep with his wife-to-be."

"Okay." Phillip put his hand out, his blunt nails grazing a fold of my shirt. "For you."

I wove my shoulder away.

"Don't do that." Something below the crossbeams of my lowest ribs clenched as I absorbed him, the chiaroscuro of his face in silhouette, his faultless smile. Nothing ever said no to those cheekbones. "You know you're supposed to ask."

"Sorry, I forgot." Glib as the first word out of a babe's milk-wet mouth, one shoulder raised then dropped.

My gaze drifted, moved until it came to rest on the fusuma. There were images of marketplaces teeming with black-lipped housewives, raccoons darting between—

I squinted. No, not raccoons. Tanuki, with their scrotums dragging behind them. Someone'd even painted the fine hairs, had made it a point to emphasize how the testes sat in their gunny sacks of tanned skin. Somehow, the profanity of the art repulsed me less than the undergrowth in which Phillip stood. The ferns grew knee-high, curled against his calves like vegetal cats.

"So, how many ghosts do you think we're going to find?" Phillip said, warming to the thought of small talk, his grin like a politician's smile beaming up from the cover of *GQ*, only better because it was actually sincere, larger than life yet still intrinsically boy next door.

"At least one." I thought about corpses. I thought about how many girls were buried beneath us, foreheads together, bodies fused in a cat's cradle of curled legs and clutching arms.

"Yeah. She's probably like the Queen of the Damned or something. I wonder what she'd look like." He undulated his hands through the air, molding his palms around the voluptuous rise and dip of an imaginary silhouette. "Bet she's hot."

A portraiture of the deceased—the owner of that voice—rose into focus in my mind's eye: a round face, wide at the cordillera of her cheekbones but otherwise gaunt, the flesh whittled by hunger and worms, her complexion waxen. Hair waterfalling ragged and black, still impaled in places by sharp golden pins.

"I don't think you can be hot after so many years dead."

"Have some imagination. Sure, the corporeal body might have suffered from decomposition. But her spiritual manifestation is probably something else."

"You're crass, Phillip." My laugh sounded wet, thick, false, forced. But Phillip didn't notice, grinning wide. I couldn't stop thinking about what might have been under his feet.

"Just a hot-blooded male," he confessed. "Doing what hot-blooded males do."

"Cute." The edge of a lip went up further than demure. "Promise me you'll rein it in."

"I promise I'll try." He fisted a hand and placed it over his heart, an admiral's salute, spine and shoulders lancing straight. That grin again, that cocksure state-funded presidential candidate smirk.

"Talk to the hand." I threw a raised palm in his direction and looked back to the fusuma. It wasn't just tanuki on exhibit. There were other yokai. It was all yokai, a veritable parade: kitsune in elaborate tomesode, tails curling with questions. Ningyo crawling from the jeweled sea. Kappa and towering oni, negotiating for baskets heaped with cucumbers. Everywhere, every last brush-painted face in sight. Even the housewives: some with eyes, some only with lips, some with gaping smiles sliced into place. Every last one of them. All fucking yokai.

"Just trying to make you laugh, Cat. That's all."

"That's what he said."

He swept his fringe from his eyes and palmed his chest with both hands, expression become grotesque with false despair. "You wound me."

"Your ego wounds you. I was just its instrument."

And he laughed then. Like it didn't matter, like it couldn't matter, not for him, not ever, not when so much of the world waited, eager, to tithe him everything for a kiss. Phillip wouldn't pauper himself with a grudge, not with the blessed largesse of his straight, white, rich-boy life.

"You're good people, Cat. You know that, right? And good people deserve happiness."

"I think that's overstating things," I told him with a half-smile for a tip. However tedious the best wishes, I couldn't fault his intent. More than anything else, I was tired. Tired of being unhappy, and even more tired of feeling sorry for the fact that I was unhappy. It was easier to agree than it was to argue, what with the immovable object that was Phillip's faith in his worldview. "But I appreciate the sentiment."

Suenomatsuyama nami mo koenamu.

A whisper, so quiet the cerebellum wouldn't acknowledge its receipt. The words were drowned by the reverb of Faiz's voice calling, an afterimage, an impression of teeth on skin. We exited the room, the future falling into place behind us. Like a wedding veil, a mourning caul. Like froth on the lip of a bride drowning on soil.

CHAPTER 2

The mansion was colossal. Bigger than it should have been. Taller. In the dregs of my mind, a voice frothed with questions: is it meant to be so big? Had I misremembered? Were all Heian houses two storeys or more?

It didn't make sense.

But here the house stood. Though only two storeys, each floor spanned at least twelve rooms and several self-contained courtyards, its symmetries united by ascetically decorated corridors. Every wall in the building was lavish with corroding artwork of the yokai: kappa and two-tailed nekomata; kitsune cowled like housewives, bartering with egrets for fresh fish. Domesticity as interpreted through the lens of the demonic.

We poured across its spaces, alone and together, sifting through the ruins. In one room sat terracotta monks, heads weighted with an ancient regret. In another, dolls with mouths lacquered black. In another, books, or at least the corpses of books. The volumes were mulch, eaten by insects, infested; edifices, turgid with egg chambers, writhed from the rot. Despite the horror of the visuals, they did not smell of anything but a green dark wetness.

The night stretched, chandeliered with fireflies and stars and the last cicada songs of the year, the world coloring indigo-dark. Music wafted from the next room: Taylor Swift and Coldplay and Carly Rae Jepsen. We'd chosen one of the ground-floor dining halls as a loci for our celebrations. There were shoji screens here—these held imagery of tengu at repose—to allow us to box-cut the space into rooms. A little privacy, we joked, for the spouses-to-be.

Backlit by torch-glow, two shadows—Phillip and Talia, I'd recognize their silhouettes anywhere—rose and entwined behind the shoji screen to our right, and Faiz, elbows-deep before in our party supplies, halted to stare. Talia's laughter flickered, girlish and eager, a darting breath of sound. I wondered then as I studied Faiz's face, the uncertainty and his pinch-mouthed worry, if he knew that Phillip and Talia had been in lust once and found myself worrying how much that answer mattered.

"You okay?" I came to his side of the room.

"Yeah. Why wouldn't I be?"

Faiz swung looks between me and the shadows on the shoji screen.

"No reason," I said. "You just seemed tense, that's all."

"Long flight."

"Uh-huh."

His head kept metronoming.

"It isn't too late to head back to Kyoto or something, you know—"

"Talia has wanted to get married in a haunted house since she was a kid. I'm not going to take that away from her." He swallowed hard between each sentence, face calcified. "Not after what it took to get us here."

"I don't want to diminish Talia's wants and dreams here but someone has to say it." I tried for a smile. "Which freaking kid grows up wanting to get married in a haunted house? I mean, *come on*."

The shadows on the other side of the shoji screen receded into tongues of slow-swaying ink, and Faiz couldn't look away.

"Cat—" Finally, Faiz tented fingers and pressed them to his nose bridge, dropped his chin. "Whatever is going on with you, you have to stop. You can't let Talia hear any of this. Do you know how much it took to convince her to let you come?"

"I know." Like rote now, my answer and the arrangement of my fingers, hands bunched and pressed to my belly, held there under the roof of my ribs. It hurt to be made to shrink like this. "I know. You've told me. I don't know. I just."

"You just what, Cat?"

I thought of the rooms and the ossuaries they'd become: the books suppurating flat-bodied beetles, hollowed, hallowed in their decay. "I think this is all a mistake. Us coming here. Us being here. I think we're going to regret it. That's all."

I walked away before Faiz could answer, could tell me again I'd been disappointing, and staggered out of the room. The air was warm, summer-wet in the plunge of the corridor. Someone'd lit a lantern at the very end, and its light bounced against a bronze mirror, my image blurred in the surface. I tensed, expecting another figure to manifest in the metal, a broken-backed body dropped over the second floor, something tall and pale and faceless.

Suenomatsuyama nami mo koenamu.

No, that wasn't right.

An image bled into place. If Phillip's ghost was real, she would be enamel and ink and a birdcage body, its bones like filigree or fish spines, barely enough to cup its impatient heart. A girl in her bridal whites, jaw sharp as a promise. Her kisses close-lipped, without tongue or heat. Like a benediction or a prayer or an ending.

And her mouth, of course, from its teeth through to the tunnel of its throat: black.

A car screamed into the dark, wheels goring the soft earth outside the house, unmooring me from that reverie. I heard the sound of mud splattering thin walls. Music pulsed through the bones of the building: not quite dubstep, frenzied, cheerfully experimental. Too excited to have ever molded the Ecstasy-glutted into shambolic choreography, but that had always been a plus point for its most strident advocate. He never liked fitting in.

Lin, I thought. He was finally here.

I couldn't let Lin see me in my previous state so I detoured to wash up, wipe the hauntings from the shadows of my eyes. Then, I went back to the appointed communal space—a room occupied by low tables and paper cranes, polka-dotted cushions we'd purchased from a yen store—to find not only Lin, but an icebox sweating on the tatami, its insides crammed with silver

Asahi cans and bottles of carbonated yuzu. A massive cast-iron pot, black and sensible, ready to be engorged with protein and vegetables.

Open Tupperware littered the rotting tables, stuffed with even more ingredients: meatballs, pork tenderloin; glistening slabs of white chicken breast; tofu, cubed and marinated; whole fish preserved in cradles of frost, eyes glimmering and silver; sirloin, short ribs, ribbons of thinly sliced beef, even cuts of marbled wagyu; daikon, bushels of spinach, napa cabbage, as many varieties of mushrooms as I could name. In the corner, separated from the main selection, were livers and fresh hearts and tripe, offal so fresh they seemed on the verge of animating.

If you're going to debauch history, go big.

"Everything's better with cheese. Come on. Let's just dump all the meat into the cheese. Make a fondue. I brought six types. Artisanal stuff. You guys appreciate the value of overpriced rotten milk, right?" Lin shook a plastic bag, bulging with trapezoid shapes, Phillip sitting cross-legged opposite.

"Cat!" He bounced onto his heels, liquid and limber. Parkour, he told me over dizzily excited emails, was becoming his new religion. It made sense, Lin confided. Martial arts shaped his past. Freerunning would direct his future. And if he was the only one who could divine the connection, well, that was hardly his error. Lin was ahead of his time, ahead of the curve, ahead of us with a Wall Street job, a Wall Street wife, a brownstone mortgage with a hydroponic herb garden on a baroque little balcony.

"Lin."

"Cat!"

But he was still my Lin, and when he crushed me to his sternum, I realized, without surprise, that I was still his Cat as well. I pressed our old name for him into his shoulder, hugging him back, breathing him in. Lin smelled of intercontinental travel: sourness under a caking of deodorant, a splash of cologne.

He pulled away, reaching an arm over my shoulder. Shadows deepened the hollows of his eyes with plum, the only outward sign of exhaustion.

"Is Faiz still in the other room?" said Talia.

We turned, six years of complicated history rolled back up and re-holstered, all for the sake of the blushing bride. Talia stood taller than all of us, mouth pinned in a line like police tape, lipstick moody against brown skin. She'd changed out of her travelling clothes into a yukata, painstakingly tailored for her frame, white moths burning to cinders on a sprawl of navy cloth. Her expression fell as they crossed my face, collapsed entirely at the sight of Lin.

"Who?" said Lin.

"He was one of your groomsmen."

"I had like sixteen groomsmen. You can't expect me to remember them all. It was an *event*, after all."

"You made him fly to Iceland." Talia thinned her mouth.

Lin draped an arm around me. "I made everyone fly to Iceland."

"He's the reason you're here. We're getting married! That's the whole point you came here!"

"Oh. That." Lin glanced at me, smirking. "I thought I was just here to see Cat."

I froze. Long enough for Talia to see and for her mouth to weigh with condolence. Lin, though, with his thoroughbred wife and his immaculate life, still blind from those late-night Manhattan lights, took no notice at all.

"He was supposed to get our surprise from the car." Talia flicked her attention to Phillip, hopeful. "We wanted to do something for you guys. Like, it's crazy that you got us a full holiday to Japan. First class too?"

I interrupted. "Technically, it was Phillip—"

"Yes, yes. Trust-fund baby paid for the bulk of it. But you all helped, you all did the very best you could. And it matters to me. To us. You have no idea." Her expression went soft, a perfect act. She flattened a palm over her heart. "So, we wanted to do something for you guys. Except that Faiz is missing his *cue*."

Enclosed in Talia's ribs was an entire vocabulary of sighs, each one layered with delicate subtleties, every laboured exhalation unique in its etymology. She raked a hand through her hair, sighed for the third, fourth time. I'd lost track at this point. Her gaze skated to mine, chagrin expressed with an arching of penciled brows. *Your fault,* declared that grim expression, no reprieve in stock.

"I'm here! Sorry!" Faiz's voice came from behind a shoji screen, quickly overshadowed by a shrill of splintering timber, worm-wounded fibres coming apart. The panel to our right shuddered before it fell over. No fanfare. No collateral damage to the adjunct architecture. Not even a pluming of grey dust. Only an audible smack as it hit the floor, a sound like a palm colliding with a cheek.

We froze like hares.

"Shit," said Faiz.

Lin was the one to break the spell. He laughed, jackal-throated and giddy. It was somehow enough. We sagged into ourselves, small talk dispensed like so much recreational Valium. Faiz stood smiling at us from behind the devastation, six-feet-but-not-quite of shame and self-loathing. He cradled a stack of slim rectangular boxes, each package wrapped in gilt, bows on every one. "Sorry."

We laughed as a group this time, and we all sounded drunk on being alive. Phillip got up and walked over to Faiz, punched the other man square in the shoulder, hard enough to dislodge his cargo. The gifts tumbled free, gloss and gold-trimmed ribbons. Phillip caught them all, naturally—one-armed and effortless—golden boy to Faiz's dross.

"This," Lin muttered with too much glee, "is how supervillains are born."

CHAPTER 3

The food was everything its aroma had vowed: decadently complex, delicious to the last sip of broth, the savoury decoction of marrow, meat, and greens almost too umami to finish. But we did. We ate until our stomachs bulged and the alcohol lost some of its effect. In between, Lin convinced us to sample his cheese, carving slivers of Danablu and jalapeño-infused Camembert for anyone who'd look at him twice. The leftovers he used to make a Hong Kong–style baked rice, melting mascarpone over pork and sweet-salty shiitake.

We devoured that too. The room laid strewn with wrapping paper. Faiz and Talia had bought us gifts: statuettes of deepest jade, the green of an ancient lake. They were each of them shaped like a woman, her head bowed as though sacralized by grief. Her legs faded into a half-finished column: she is being buried alive, buried by a lord's hope, buried to hold steady the weight of her master's manor.

Hitobashira.

I stroked a restless thumb over my effigy's cheek. There were neither eyes nor mouth on her, no way for her to scream or see. How'd they known to gather these? I wondered. The trip was billed as a surprise. Had Talia known? Had Phillip, our golden boy, god-king of small towns, perfect Phillip who no woman would reject, coyly spoken to Talia beforehand?

"We should play a game," Talia purred, eyes lidded and drowsy with mischief, crooking her fingers at Faiz. He stood up and went from lantern to lantern, extinguishing their flames. Our shadows arched to the ceiling. "It's called Hyakumonogatari Kaidankai."

"Excuse me?" said Lin.

"Hyakumonogatari Kaidankai," Talia repeated, pronunciation paced for intelligibility. She looked at me then, really looked, harpooning my attention with the steadiness of her regard. "A Gathering of One Hundred Ghost Stories. I think?"

"Or weird stories," said Faiz.

"Ancient samurai started this game as a kind of parlour game to see who the bravest of them were. They'd light one hundred candles in the room. Each samurai would tell a ghost story, extinguishing a candle at the end, and the winner would be whoever survived the ordeal without flinching."

"Or going to the bathroom?" said Lin.

"Uh. Sure," said Faiz.

"So, what's the point of the whole ritual anyway?" said Lin.

Talia was on her feet now too, walking a reverse circuit from her fiancé, her shadow growing longer as she extinguished the lanterns limning the parabola of her route.

Until at last there was one lantern remaining, its flame twitching, throwing shapes over the walls. From up the stairs, candlelight fell unevenly.

"What do you think?" Talia's smile was sly. "To make a place where spirits would be welcome. Now, come on."

We went up. Someone had lit one hundred red candles in a room that must have belonged to a second wife, a concubine who had lost her lustre, a room too small and too spare to have homed someone who mattered, a chapel sacred to the incidental. If the owner was ever beloved, it was grudgingly, resentfully: an act of reluctant duty. The room's only grace was an oval mirror, taller than plausible, its frame made of black ceramic, seamed with gold arteries.

"This isn't creepy at all," said Phillip.

"You talking about the room, the ceremony, or the fact that Talia packed a hundred candles in her bag without any of us noticing?" said Lin after a quick glance around him, Talia nowhere in immediate sight.

"All of it?" Phillip's reflection had no face, just a thumbprint on the bronze mirror. It could have belonged to anyone, anything else. "Like, this feels unholy."

"And the fact you could purchase access to a historical site without having to fill out any kind of paperwork didn't?" Lin drawled, shoulder laid against a pillar, no color to the latter any longer, not unless ancient was a hue. "If there's anything unholy, it's the heights that rich white men—"

"I knew I shouldn't have taken time to fill you in. And come on, it's not like I'm doing it for myself."

"You're doing it for Talia, I know," said Lin.

A beat that went too long. "And Faiz too."

"You're still sweet on her, aren't you?" said Lin, face cracked into a grin. He pushed from the wall.

"Jesus hell, Lin," I said.

"What?" He threw a shrug, hands tossed up so quickly that his fingers, if they had been birds, would have broken in the violence. "We're all thinking it. The stupid little figurines that Talia gave us. This was supposed to be a surprise elopement. How did she know, dude? Come on. Tell me."

Phillip moved fast. Faster than I think any of us could have gambled he'd go even with his quarterback history. With that much muscle, you expected to see the machinery move: his physique bunching for motion, creating momentum. But Phillip poured across the room: six gliding steps and Lin suddenly was pincered between him and a wall, head ricocheting from the impact.

"The fuck are you doing?" I shouted, lunging for Phillip's arm.

He glared at me then. And his eyes were cold, so cold your heart would freeze in that blue.

"You're right," he said. Phillip, we all knew, had his universal script. "I'm above that."

"But not above sleeping with someone else's wife." Lin collared his own neck with a hand and rubbed his Adam's apple after Phillip had let him go, smile enduring as a bad habit.

"I didn't sleep with Talia."

"Sure," said Lin, strolling out then—*finally*—and the house devoured his footsteps. Silence leaned into us, a conspiring friend. I looked up at Phillip. He stood stooped with two fists balled-up at his sides, teeth gritted, breath bleeding in trails.

"Hey."

A sidelong look but no sound yet otherwise.

"Hey," I said again. "The fuck was that?"

His rage began to slough as he spoke. "I don't know. I lost my temper. That asshole does it to me all the time. I think I can keep my shit together but something about Lin just makes me want to punch a wall."

Phillip wiped his tongue along the edge of a tooth, hands raised for me to see, the palms cut with half-moons from his nails.

"You know that's what he's like, though."

"I don't know how you put up with him." Phillip kept going, his internal monologue, as always, so loud it couldn't ever make space for collaboration. "He's a piece of shit."

"Is he right, though?"

"What?"

"Is he right?" I said, and the house breathed in, swallowing half the candles, making a mess of the dark. "About you and Talia."

"You sound like you want it to be," came the reply, too slow for it to be innocent of Lin's insinuations, air filtered through Phillip's teeth in a languid hiss. At least there was no more anger, that part of him thankfully exhumed. His countenance, badly lit, was grave but harmless.

"I don't have an opinion on this."

"Why'd you ask?"

"Because you nearly beat someone to death over it."

"It didn't have anything to do with that. Like I said, it's just Lin gets under my skin." He exhaled, tectonic in its release. "I should go apologize to him, though. You're right. I don't fucking know what came over me."

I said nothing until Phillip's footsteps died away, and then turned, and I—

Suenomatsuyama nami mo koenamu.

A female voice, solicitous and sweet. Distantly, the brain stem screeched, stress hormones wailing at my motor system, demanding I run, run now, escape into the sanctuary of multiplicity, disappear into the waiting herd, do anything so long as I remove myself from probable harm, anything just go, go now.

But my limbs would not concede to their urging.

Suenomatsuyama nami mo koenamu.

She—I pictured a girl, smaller than me, younger, black hair pouring from a widow's peak—repeated, this time with more insistence. I felt molars close over my earlobe, felt a tongue trace its circumference. Her breath was damp, warm.

Suenomatsuyama nami mo koenamu.

What. The word pebbled in my throat, cold and dead. Haltingly, head full of static, I lurched stiff-legged towards the mirror. This was a dream. This was not a dream. This was a haunting, a possession, and any second now, I'd cut my throat, the first casualty of the night.

After all, isn't that the foremost commandment in the scripture of horror? They who are queer, deviant, tattooed, tongue-pierced Other must always die first. The slurred remnants of my consciousness chewed on the thought as my eyes slid across the mirror, my stomach clenched.

So many thoughts. None of them anything but a knee-jerk distraction.

I stared into the brass and there she was, Jesus fuck. Standing behind me, chin braced against my shoulder, arms laced around my waist. Fingers snarled in my shirt, their grip possessive. She was so close, yet somehow, I couldn't make out her face.

No.

That wasn't right.

My vision was just fine. It was my brain. My brain wouldn't inventory its observations, would not process and sustain any memory of her face, retain anything but the red of her rosebud mouth, the lacquered black of her hair. Her hands moved. Her fingers sunk into the grooves between my ribs, squeezed. I gasped at the pressure and, in answer, she made animal noises, soothing and sweet. The light plunged through the gap between her lips, and there was only ink and the smell of vinegar, only

black

teeth.

"Cat?"

I jolted. I was back where I'd originally been standing, diagonal to the mirror, no dead woman holding me to her breast. Not even a sheen of sweat on my skin to tell you I'd been scared out of my mind. Just silence and the mildewed heat, the taste of the room sitting heavy as altar bread, ashen and stale and oversweet.

"You okay?" Talia leaned her weight against the doorway, arms crossed, a hundred sentences suspended between each syllable, most saliently this: *what the fuck are you doing?* No real animosity, however. Talia's too cultured for that. But that perennial caginess because you can dress a pig in diamonds but it'll still drown itself in slop first chance it gets. No matter how often Talia smiled at me, she did not want me here.

"You were staring at the wall."

"Was I?"

That slimming of her mouth again and when she spoke, it wasn't with her satin polish, bitterness coarsening up her tone. "You know, we don't have to like each other but you don't have to be a bitch."

Bitch is the kind of word that reads like a gunshot, rings like a punch. I snapped straight at the sound, the world clarified again: distant warm candle-glow and Talia's glacial stare. "What is your problem with me? And I mean besides the one I already know."

"My problem is that you can't even answer a question without trying to be a smartass."

"Hate to break it to you but I'm not trying to be smart, I am—"

"See? That's what I mean. I asked you if you were okay. That was all. And you couldn't even answer that without some kind of goddamned wisecrack."

"Did you actually mean it?"

"What?"

"Did you actually mean it?"

"The fuck are you talking about?" Talia gawked at me. "What are you even talking about now?"

I could see why Lin defaulted to wit where he could. Easier to run your mouth, run from the Sisyphean work that was being emotionally open. Easier not to think about *her* and what my brain mutinied from remembering about the girl in the mirror. I trailed fingers along the roof of my head, patted down my hair, and smiled. "Your concern about whether I'm okay. Did you mean that?"

"Fuck me." Shoot and score. "That's what I get for trying to be nice to you."

"That's what you get for being fake."

"What do you want from me?" Her voice brittled. "I'm trying for Faiz. I don't like you and I don't think that I'm an asshole for it. You tried to break us up. But you know what? I'm working on that. I would trade a lot of money for you to not be here but this is where we are. Fucking meet me halfway."

"If it helps, I wish you weren't here either."

"I hope the house eats you." Talia, her charity only good for so much.

"I hope the same about you."

CHAPTER 4

"Whose turn is it?"

"Not it." Lin lobbed a kernel of caramel popcorn upwards, missed its descent by a millimeter. It bounced off his nose and rolled under a shelf. Fat-faced dolls in ragged magistrate wear, chignons still sleek, watched us from beside princesses in full jūnihitoe, cascades of emerald and golden damask, their brows dewed with brass. I stared as a fly hatched from the husk of a boy's small porcelain skull. Of all the figurines, this was the only one to have not survived time's touch. It looked like someone'd grabbed him by the jaw, squeezed until the cheekbones snapped, fracturing inwards. A sacrifice.

The thought filled me like ice water.

The dolls—an audience of dozens, set on thin shelves—stayed silent as Talia padded back inside from wherever she had been, their hands on their thighs, suspended on the brink of breath. It was late enough to lose track of the hours to exhaustion. Talia made us parade through every room until we found this one. This one because the last six lacked the right atmosphere. I'd thought it was stupid at first. But as we told stories of drowned things and hungry ones, it started to make sense. There was power here, even if it was of our own invention.

We killed a candle with every story until there was one last flickering survivor. Its light twitched through the shoji screen. The walls here frothed with waves and rough ocean. Through its lambent waters, the paint glittering as though tinctured with crushed sapphire, woodblock octopi watched us incuriously.

"I'll do it." I flipped my phone onto its screen, pounded down the last Asahi, chasing down the thin, flat flavor with Lin's plum wine. My teeth were just sugar now, furred with so much plaque I couldn't stop working my tongue over them, over and over. Like a horse. Like a dog that'd gotten into a bag of toffee. Back. Forth. Back. Forth. "I've got a story."

Faiz spoke up first. Sometimes, he still remembered how to be a best friend. "You don't have to. You've had a rough night. Just sit and enjoy—"

My vision gyred, one way and then another. I'd

drunk too much. I didn't care. I swayed upright onto my feet, bracing against a shelf. "No, no. I'm okay. I've got a story. Blow the rest of your shit out of the water."

"I don't know. Faiz's one about his ex's uncle was pretty good. Makes me never want to go back—" said Lin.

"Ssh." I pushed a finger to Lin's mouth. Shadows frescoed the corners of the room, elongated its angles, bent them into nightmare bodies. Bile soured the back of my throat and I swallowed against the coming hangover. I was sick of this. Sick of everything. "Ssh."

The world swung.

"Sit down."

"You going to tell me to go fetch next?"

"Jesus." Faiz got up, grabbed a water bottle, tipped its neck at me. "You're drunk, Cat. Sit down before—"

"I make a fool of myself?"

"He didn't mean it like that." No break between Faiz fucking up and Talia stepping to the plate, cause and effect, the two synthesized into one perfect choreography. I hated them for that. This wasn't how any of it was supposed to go.

"I've known Faiz—" I strangled the rest of the sentence and sat down again, a knot of acid sizzling just under where my ribs fork from my sternum, like chapel doors or a wishbone. *I've known Faiz since before the thought of fucking him was a wet spot in your crotch.* I gulped down vomit, two fingers bolted over my lips. "Just let me tell my story."

Phillip exhaled. "Christ."

"Fine," Talia said, while Faiz continued standing, looking like he had at least another paragraph left to recite. But he gave in, stroking his fingers through Talia's hair as he lowered himself beside her, knees bumping. He wouldn't compromise on hydration, however, wouldn't stop bobbing the bottle in my direction until I snatched the container and took a swig.

The water went down like a swallow of light. "Okay, okay. Let's do this. Once upon a time."

You know how poets say sometimes that it feels like the whole world is listening?

It was just like that.

Except with a house instead of an auditorium of academics, collars starched, textbooks like scriptures, each chapter color-coded by importance. The manor inhaled. It felt like church. Like the architecture had dulled its heartbeat so it could hear me better, the wood warping, curling around the room like it was a womb, and I was a new beginning. Dust sighed from the ceiling. Spiderwebs fell in umbilical cords, a drape of silver.

It felt like the house talking to me through the mouths of moths and woodlice, the creak of its foundations, the little black summer ants chewing through what remained of our food like we'd left bodies, not balled-up, slickly gleaming cling wrap. The air smelled of raw meat, lard, and bits of seared protein.

I hoped to hell in that moment that *she* was listening.

Half because I was tired of being unloved, being pitied like a fawn panting its last handful of breaths into a ditch. Half because I hoped it was all true.

A little bit of magic.

Even if it was hungry.

Even if it was a house with rotting bones and a heart made out of a dead girl's ghost, I'd give it everything it wanted just for scraps. Some unabridged attention, some love.

Even if it was from a corpse with blackened teeth.

Anything to feel alive again right now.

Suenomatsuyama nami mo koenamu.

I'm so tired of this, I thought. Come make me warm and I'll give you what we both want.

"Once upon a time," I repeated. "Once upon a time, there was a house in the middle of the forest and it stood silently until a group of twentysomethings barged through the door, looking for ghosts."

Phillip and Faiz gave each other high-fives.

"They ate their dinner. They drank their beer. They

played a game to call up the dead from their rest. Except they didn't have to. The house already knew they were there." I sloped backwards, weight balanced on the heels of my palms, watched that one fly as it wiggled from a crack in the ceramic boy's skull and buzzed to another doll, squeezing through its black-lipped mouth. I thought I could hear its feet scratch at the lacquer.

Lin caught on first. "Did you see something?"

"A girl," I whispered. It should have sounded like a joke, something stupid. But a wind frissoned through the cracks in the shoji and it was as if the manor was laughing, I was sure, its voice dripping with termites. "A pale little bride with a smile full of ink."

Right on cue, all the lights went out.

—⁊ᛁᚴ—

"Shit!"

Smartphones strobed to life, slicing the darkness into halves, quarters, polygons of irregular sizes like pieces of shattered glass. Phillip staggered upright, an arm raised to fence the group from the door. "What the fuck was that?"

"Probably just a breeze." Lin didn't sound so sure, though, body thrumming with adrenaline, and you could just about see his heart battering against his breastbone, dying to get out. He was afraid. I couldn't wrap my alcohol-addled brain around the idea. Lin was never afraid. But since he was, it meant that the rest of us should have already started running.

I lapped my tongue over my upper lip.

"It's her."

Talia's eyes shone in the near dark. "What are we waiting for? Let's check it out."

She clambered onto her feet, swayed for one tight-rope of a heartbeat, before the momentum drove her straight into a sprint. Talia was out the door before the rest of us could put together why forward was the wrong direction, before Faiz could wring out a desperate "Wait!" and take off after her, the rest of us clattering along behind. All of us shouting, filling up the corridors with our voices, and somewhere, an ohaguro-bettari was wandering the house her husband built.

I came out of the room in time to see Talia flashing down a corridor, her silhouette receding along the wall, spotlighted by the halogen glare of her phone. No foot-steps, their escape frictionless as envy. I started forward, only to be jerked back, Lin hauling me back inside, my wrist trapped in his long fingers.

"Wait," he hissed. "It isn't safe."

"Don't you think I know? There's something wrong with this place."

"Well, shit. Yeah. It's a giant mansion in the middle of nowhere full of dolls and creepy shit." Sweat gleamed on his forehead, dampened the ring of his collar. I tugged, but Lin wouldn't let go. He adjusted his grip instead, wrapped his palm tighter around my joint. His wedding ring ground into bone.

"And this is safer? Separating from the group?"

"From those idiots? Absolutely." He craned a look outside, neck rigid. Phillip and Faiz were wading farther into the house, their voices gusting together into one unbroken howl, one throat. "Structurally speaking, this place is a shithole. Who knows if it's going to come down on our heads? What with all that stomping—"

"You're deflecting." I pulled again.

"Yeah? So what if I am."

"They're our friends. We have to go after—"

"Your friends." Lin yanked. With one supple motion, his hands routed my arms into improbable configurations and pinned them there, two degrees from torture. I tested his hold anyway, winced as my synapses lit up with a *what-the-fuck-had-you-expected*. "Not mine. I don't give a shit about those idiots."

I bared my teeth. "Nice. Real nice. Those were your groomsmen."

"I had a baker's dozen, so whatever. There'd be spare. But that isn't the fucking point." He nuzzled his head against my temple, exhaled. "Cat, this is literally the part where the supporting cast dies horribly. You're bisexual. I'm the comic relief. It's going to be one of us."

"But—"

"Phillip's white. He'll be fine. Faiz's the hero so he won't die in the first fucking act. And Talia's, well, maybe Talia's thoroughly fucked. But I don't care about her." He said it so casually. Like it was the easiest line in the universe, simpler even than *hey, how ya doing, I didn't miss you at my wedding at all, and I'll never ask why you didn't RSVP, didn't stop to tell me your world was crashing down.*

I kept rotating my shoulders, checking to see if I could find any give, any way to move without dislocating my elbow, or ripping the tissue threading my scapula together. And all that's assuming, of course, that Lin wouldn't let go if push escalated to shove. I leaned into a direction and counted how long it took before the amygdala called time-out on my chicanery, flashbangs of pain going off over my corneas like a black-and-white Fourth of July.

Three seconds.

"Let go."

I couldn't hear the others anymore, but the floorboards throbbed like they had a heart carved into their grain.

Lin held on. "God damn it, Cat. I'm not the enemy."

Four, five.

I loaded a breath into my lungs like it was a silver bullet, the air burning between my teeth. Six. Seven. Eight. Between every second, I eased another millimeter forward, let myself slide between the sine waves of pain, Lin's grasp slackening in increments. At that point, it was just about ego, mine and his, daring each other to break.

"Cat—"

The fusuma opposite us rolled open, rocketing so hard along the walls it slammed into the wall.

We jumped, Lin nearly torquing my hand the wrong way. It was Talia, a shoulder leaned against the frame, the mass of her hair squirming around her face, her eyes black. The light from our phones were three xenon squares, mirrored in each pupil. She grinned at us. "You wouldn't believe what I found."

My breath shallowed to sips.

Something was wrong.

It wasn't just the fact that Talia had bolted so unexpectedly out of that door, although that was at least some of it. It was the way she did it. No matter how many times I turned the thought over, looking for a new angle, the same image kept coming up: a fishing line rolled down her throat, tracing the ripples of her intestinal tract, the hook at its end crooking up and out through her navel, bent like a finger calling her onward.

"What'd you find?" The corridor behind her peeled away into a hell of opened doors, closing into a deep indigo murk. Something was wrong. Somewhere, choking in alcohol and stress hormones, there was a piece of me that knew why.

"You wouldn't believe it. Seriously. Like, oh my god—"

"Was it the ghost girl?" Lin interrupted.

"No. Shit. I wish. But it's almost as good. I can't believe—" Talia strained her hair through her fingers and rubbed the ends together. Her expression was exultant. "You have to see it."

Phillip loped out of the gloom, his smartphone bleaching his blond hair to cartilage colors, his skin to polished bone china. A second later, Faiz came up from behind, his breath thready, whistling between his teeth as he shambled to where Talia stood, the look on her face halfway between worship and a woman's love for her dog.

Faiz walked up to her and they sank together into an embrace. I glanced away, an itching in the skin below my right eye. The muscle fluttered. My head swam, full of static again, like someone'd tuned the inside of my head to a broadcast decades dead.

"Why the hell did you run off like that? What were you thinking?"

"Sorry. I know. I just—I was excited."

Faiz, shouting: "You could have been hurt!"

"I know, I know." Talia waved away his concern, her eagerness a knife working under all of our jabber, all of our fears, cutting away the parts that didn't fit what she needed. Feverish. "I'm sorry. But seriously, it's fine. Nothing happened. It's all good. And it doesn't matter. I need you to follow me. You have to see this."

Lin's fingers met with mine, familiar. I ran my eyes over the lacquered rail along which the fusuma had moved, crossed it to where it met with the adjoining wall before I flicked my gaze to the opposite end. There weren't any hinges.

No grooves, no indentations, no clever mechanism to accommodate the moving panels. The rail looked ornamental, was ornamental.

It didn't make sense.

"No offense to the happy couple here." Lin coughed into his free hand. "But assuming that there's something actually here, how the fuck do we know that Talia isn't possessed by some crazy—"

"There wasn't a door," I said.

It had been a wall. It was still a wall. But no one

seemed to conjecture the problem save for me, and no one was *listening*.

"How did you get in there? There wasn't a door."

"What are you talking about?" Talia laced an arm around Faiz's, full of absolvement for my outburst, chin tipped to a modest angle. She rocked the fusuma back and forth. "It's right here."

"But it wasn't there a second ago. We went through every room on this floor and the one below. That door didn't exist. The hallways. All of it. It didn't exist when we first came in."

"You're drunk," said Talia.

"Please don't go with her," I said, starting forward.

Lin folded his arm around my shoulders. "I got her. You do what you want."

"You can't go in there."

Phillip started towards Lin and me, palm turned up. "We shouldn't leave these—"

"We're fine." Lin bared a snarl. "You guys go do protagonist shit."

"Come on." Talia wrapped both Faiz and Phillip in smiles, a hand in each of hers, and walked them into the mouth of the house.

"There w-n't a door. They neesh to come back. They arsh goin' to get themselves killed. Fuck." It wouldn't come out right: the words muffled, my tongue suddenly too big, a nerveless flap of muscle, stringing sick onto the floor.

"It's fine. It's just a stupid old house." Lin rubbed absent circles into the muscles bracketing my spine, right where the brain stem eases into the neck. "They're going to come back spooked and that's it. Chill."

The words came together, but I swallowed them stillborn. It was too esoteric, too ambiguous to get across. Maybe I'd been wrong.

But if I wasn't . . .

I got up, Lin bellowing protests, and staggered after the clack of sandals on wood, half-blind as I followed my Dantes into damnation.

CHAPTER 5

He caught me by the nape of my collar as I stumbled onto a bridge, its blackwood railings corniced by sculptures of maidens in repose, their bodies twisted around one another, so that at a glance, they resembled a strange garden. Below: an ornamental pond rendered tar-dark and fathomless. How had we gotten here? We'd been above ground level. But the doors had opened nonetheless to lightless sky and cold air.

"The fuck, Cat. The fuck. No. We're not—"

"They were there for me when you weren't." I blotted tears from my eyes, slowing, thought for a moment on the value of pointing out what had happened as the world smeared into a sodium haze. Somehow, Lin had taken no notice of the spatial weirdness so I said nothing.

We were fucked, clearly. Might as well die without any bad blood. "They kept me going. They got me to come out of the house. They made me feel normal."

"Well, if you'd just called me—"

"You didn't even tell me you were getting married." The words melted together, no syllabic definition, just sound: awkward and delicate. "You have no idea how much that part *bugged* me."

Lin winced like he'd been slapped, staggering to a stop, fingers spasming. A slight tug on my collar, as though that would be enough to rewind everything, replace it with something better. Pull me back from the ledge, put down the knife, undo the hurt that curled its cold finger around the trigger.

"I didn't think you'd want to know."

"Why?" Just a whisper in the autumn-blued air, one word, the sound of it raw and desperate. Moonlight seeped through cuts in the trees, striping his cheek like wounds scratched across my thigh.

"Because you were so unhappy."

"Is that why you didn't visit me either? Didn't reach out?" The words swayed like a body on a rope, finally slack. Emotional distance reframing that previous in-carnation as a stranger, without body or nuance, a monochrome despair decanted into the slumped mouth, a six-month affair with cigarettes and self-loathing. I

wasn't that person, couldn't possibly be, and the even-
ness in my voice had to be testimony to the fact. "You
could have said something. You could have been there
for me. Instead, you went and . . . I don't know. I have
no idea what I'm trying to say anymore. Life's kinda
messy, isn't it?"

"I'm sorry I wasn't there." Every part of that sentence ached through its recital.

"It's not your fault. You're allowed happy." I shed
my hoodie, tossed it into the pool below us. The algae,
clumping filthily around the bulrush, kept the garment
from sinking, and something else floated it away. A fish
broke the surface tension, gasping, green clinging to its
lips. "It really isn't. You don't have to—look, this isn't
about that. I'm just trying to make a point. These guys
kept me from doing anything too stupid. So, I owe them.
Kind of."

Close enough. There wasn't time for anything else.

The nature of my announcement pressed down, and
I watched for a long minute as the light sieved from his
face. He swallowed. I reached out and bent my forehead
to his.

"I was scared and stupid and, frankly, selfish. I
just . . ."

"You came back and that's what is important. We're
friends again."

"I'm still sorry," Lin said, threading his fingers with mine. "It—"

"It's okay. You're here now. But we gotta go. Now." This time, Lin didn't argue.

─◦◦─

By the time we found them, Talia was all dressed up in someone else's wedding clothes.

She looked radiant in the dim hall into which Lin and I stepped, illuminated by the lantern set down at her sandaled feet. Her jūnihitoe was sumptuous, palatial in architecture, every single color from the palette of a perfect dawn, each drape of silk embroidered with faces from a children's book, glimmering with reflected candle-glow. Against the vermillion of the overcoat, Talia's skin seemed depthless. Not brown, but black as ink on teeth.

"Where the fuck—" Lin wasn't smiling for once, no attempt to defuse, disarm. "You know what? Doesn't fucking matter. You know this probably belonged to a dead person, right?"

"The hell is wrong with you?" Faiz trotted out from a side room, wearing executioner blacks: a regular suit, slightly rumpled, bowtie and everything. "If you're going to be an asshole, get out."

"Sorry," Lin said, not sounding like he was at all. "Just pointing out the obvious."

Faiz pinched his brow. "You two are drunk idiots."

I slid down to a knee, gritted my teeth against the headache painting lights behind my eyes. "This is a mistake."

"Are you talking about the ghost girl?" Phillip circled around from behind me, cupped me below the arms, and lifted me straight up, propped me against an alcove where a vase blooming with dead flowers sat. The petals crumbled to ashes as I leaned back. The air tasted like honey, had a chewiness to it. "No one's seen her. Don't worry."

No. Not like honey, I corrected myself. It was sinewy, sweet as a knot of tendon after you'd gnawed on it for minutes, a faintly corrupt delight. "We need to go."

"After the ceremony," said Phillip.

"We need to go," I said again.

"It'll be fine."

"Spoken like a true white guy." Lin rolled a frustrated noise in his throat, entirely animal. Ahead of us, Faiz and Talia joined shy hands in front of an altar to the faded dead, the small gods of whatever still lived in the eaves. You could feel the house pull in a breath. You could feel its eyes. I could. "Ignoring everything that Cat's said, how does any of this seem like a good idea?

Even—even assuming that it's all just the delusions of an incredibly drunk mind, this is just plain weird. How the fuck does any of this make sense to you people?"

"You know—" Talia sighed.

Lin, always so happy to rephrase everything as a joke, sucked at the air, before the words came out in a shotgun blast. "Fuck you and everything you think you know."

"You're welcome to leave. The only person who wanted you here was Cat, and the two of you—" She bit her lip as I stood, teeth a wound of white. Untangling from Faiz, Talia surged forward, red silk worming behind her. "Just. Get out, will you? No one wanted you here. Not you, not your jokes, your stupid goddamned cheese—"

"Hey. You ate as much of my rice as anyone else, thank you very much."

"Go," Talia said, one last time with feeling. "Just. Go away."

"Fine," I said.

Everyone turned as I spoke. Every eye in the hall including the ones dotting the walls, the ones framed in gold-leaf, drawn in brushstrokes. The room spun, wobbled on the fulcrums of a thousand painted faces.

And the manor breathed out.

"We're leaving," I said, and then once more for good

measure, softer the second time around. "We're leaving."

"Cat, don't." Faiz was already cutting in. "You don't have to go. We don't have any problem with you. It's just. Lin, dude. Sorry. No hard feelings. But I'd like this to be a happy thing, you know? Just. Can you take—actually, I don't know, you know?"

"They can both go, if they want," said Talia.

"Talia." Phillip, intervening at last, a clergy's bright collar buttoned to his cassock, every inch the Hollywood caricature. Neither Talia nor Faiz were Catholic, but the joke had been that it didn't matter. This whole thing was meant to be nondenominational, nonorthodox. A gift wrapped up in a joke, wrapped up in an experience. "Is this really what you want for your wedding? I don't think kicking Lin out of—"

Talia tweaked her veil into place: an anachronism, a concession to media indoctrination by the West. It was a scrap of white lace, so gaudy against her borrowed raiments, threaded with something that made it gleam in the light. The tasseled curtain came down with a sigh of silver.

The lights twitched.

"Don't need your pity," I said, stiffly. "Don't want it either."

"Cat. You're drunk," Phillip said, and his kindness

had a kind of teeth to it, had subtitles. Sit the hell down, it said. The walls wore a senate of kitsune, pale-furred, the tips of their tails dip-dyed in coal. They waited, uncharacteristically imperious. A delegation of tengu was bringing their prime minister a gift.

"What happened to trying to keep these idiots alive?" said Lin.

"Like he said, I'm drunk." My laugh was just bones knocking together, without any meat to cushion their clamor. Hateful, hollow. I gritted my teeth against their stares, began limping back towards the door. "I don't know better. I'm tired."

"You don't have to go," Faiz said again. Like that'd be exactly enough to make it all better, put me back on my leash. He said it with so much sympathy too. Too much, in fact, his expression greasy with it. And I stared at him, I could see where that compassion slopped away to reveal exasperation, irritation, disgust as old as the memory of us first exchanging hellos in school. "Really."

I ignored him. "Come on, Lin."

"Cat." Faiz, still trying. Too little, too late.

I didn't look back.

Footsteps charted the mathematics of their motions: a drag of fabric as Talia swept around the bell curve of her orbit, Faiz's plodding shuffle falling a quarter-beat behind. Phillip's footsteps crisp but hesitant, loud on the wood. Lin was the only one who moved like he wasn't weighted down by sins, nearly noiseless as he padded along behind me.

Halfway:

"You know what? Fuck it."

That was all the warning we were given. Lin's stride became a run, and I turned in time to see him lunging for Talia's veil. His fingers closed over the pearlescent gauze, the beaded trim. The fabric tore in ripples, like swathes of pale skin, sunlight gleaming through, soft as eyelashes. Lin's cry of triumph choked to death halfway to its birth.

She hid nothing this time, the thing beneath Talia's veil. My girl from the mirror. There wasn't a face to remember because there wasn't a face to find. Black hair tendriled across contourless meat, no features to be seen. Only suggestions. Only smooth flesh and that grinning mouth, those red lips stretched as far as they'd go, black teeth, and the smell of ink. As I gawked, Talia's kimono bled itself of color, pinks and golds runneling from every layer, pouring into the dust at her feet so all that was left was white, the color of expensive chalk and bone left to cook in the sun.

The ohaguro-bettari began to laugh before any of us could think to scream.

CHAPTER 6

Who the—what the fuck is that?"

Faiz made a noise that I've never heard, a whining sound that hitched in his lungs, expressed in gasps. The kitsunes turned. No more pretenses now. Painted tengu approached in staccato, ticking across the seams in the shoji, a stop-motion flock, their expressions mocking. Faiz hit the floor, crab-walked about two feet backwards, gargling obscenities in a throat that wouldn't work.

Phillip crossed himself the wrong way three times before he looked over, eyes so wide that both irises were necklaced in white. Outside the room, through cracks in the walls and in the few places where the lantern-light would reach, I could see movement, subtle and swaying.

"Told you she was probably going to be possessed and everything was going to hell," Lin said, more satisfied, maybe, than anyone had a right to be.

The dead girl, the thing in Talia's place, Faiz's changeling bride, white as a tongue of wax, let her laughter ebb to a giggle, low and coquettish. Demurely, she raised a sleeve to her mouth, her chin ducked, and moved towards Faiz, each of her steps causing a scramble back of his. He whimpered, head lolling.

"Suenomatsuyama nami mo koenamu."

"What the fuck is it saying?" Faiz whispered hoarsely.

"Dude, seriously. We're both Chinese. Don't know what Phillip is." Lin jerked a thumb at the other man, voice thinned by hysteria. "But you're the only one with a Japanese parent."

"Something about a mountain." I swallowed, too petrified to correct him. I spoke the language too, if barely at this point, the knowledge leeched by crisis. "A-a promise?"

"That's helpful." Phillip thumbed through his phone and whatever dregs of satellite data he could milk from the air, face contorted. His hands shook. "I've got a— shit, the fucking page won't load. Why won't this—ah, fuck."

"Suenomatsuyama nami mo koenamu," said the dead bride again, this time with no musicality, her delivery urgent, her voice abraded, like she'd spent too long screaming in the dark.

Then a memory filled my mouth: "If I were one that had a heart that would cast you aside and turn to someone else, then waves would rise above the pines of Seunomatsu Mountain."

"What the fuck are you talking about?" demanded Lin.

"That's the poem. The thing she keeps repeating. It's part of the poem," I said. "She's still waiting for her husband-to-be. After all these years, she's hanging on to the hope he's coming home."

"That or she's saying it ironically," declared Lin. "Which, I can tell you now, worries me because that sounds like the recipe for an angry fucking ghost."

He paused.

"Or angry ghost fucking."

I bayed my laughter, sudden and delirious. At the sound, Phillip's phone slid from his trembling fingers, cracked open on the floorboard. Glass shimmered. The ohaguro stopped, a broken wind-up toy. No breath, no shiver of muscle, candlelight washing golden blue over enamel skin.

"Fuck," Phillip repeated and we all stared as one at our ghost.

She chittered and the kitsune in the walls answered,

applauding in perfect silent synchronicity, their fur flushing burgundy from nose to curling tails. Their eyes grew cataracted, a film of silk. I couldn't stop staring. Then, the ohaguro began to laugh.

"Where's Talia?" Faiz whispered.

The ohaguro stopped and, jerkily, she cocked her head.

"Where's Talia? Where the fuck is Talia? Where is she you fucking—" Faiz choked down that last word, but the swallowed *bitch* still hissed through the air. He stumbled upright, slipped on sweat, nostrils and mouth and eyes dripping clear mucus, a slickness pearling along his chin. "Give her back. Give. Her. Back."

The words stuttered together, warping with agony. Over and over and over, until he'd tortured the meaning from the refrain, until it was a croak hollowed out of his belly. *Give her back. Give her back. Giveherback. Giverakgiverakgiverak.*

"Jesus, man. What do you—" Phillip started.

Faiz hit her.

His fist bore into her sternum, through it. But there was no crunch, no wet pop of bone concaving, no sound to speak of. Nothing but softness, the ohaguro's body bending into the impact, swallowing his arm to the elbow. For a moment, I thought she might have a mouth buried in the mound of white silk, that we were a sliver of a breath away from hearing Faiz scream himself bloody.

But he only stared at her.

"Please."

She stroked his cheek with the back of her alabaster hand, wove her fingers beneath his jaw, slid her thumb across his lips before popping the digit into his parted mouth. I thought I saw his tongue move, see Faiz suckle at the extremity, red muscle laving over her pale, pale skin. That laugh again. Girlish, gorged with knowing. The rest of us stood rooted, transfixed by the obscene tableau.

"Please," Faiz moaned around the curve of her thumb.

The ohaguro vanished.

⸙

But the kitsune stayed.

The tengu did too.

The ceiling ripened with bodies, yokai bleeding from the other rooms to come gawk; first oozing through the cracks in the architecture, slithering rills of wet ink, before regaining three-dimensionality. They leered at us from the wood and the paper, faces and palms pressed against what now felt like a sheeting of glass. It was as though we stood in a vivarium, had always stood in display, surrounded by children but unconscious to that truth until now.

But even that impression gave way.

Slowly, as more painted bodies—some no more than scrawled lines, others magnificently detailed—crowded the ceiling, it began to distend, almost as if it had turned gelatinous. Under a pustular overhang of grinning onlookers, our group turned to each other.

"Now what?" Lin demanded.

Faiz sat keening into his hands, a broken howl that wouldn't stop or waver, no matter which of us came over to whisper platitudes into his ear. He convulsed with his misery, scratched at his cheeks until the skin tore into translucent ribbons, embedding itself under his nails. Blood ran in thick stripes, muddying his hands.

"I don't know," I said, chugging water. The taste of it made me think of the pond, of algae and silt and bodies, bellies curdle-pale and soft, curving out of the murk. Wide piscine eyes flashing beneath the surface, silvery with mucus. I gagged and spat petals of duckweed, slick tangles of black hair. "What the—"

"Looks like we hit critical mass for supernatural stuff." Lin giggled, high and weird. I winced at his pitch, each burst of lunatic laughter like a nail pounded through my temple.

"Stop it," I said.

No one listened to me. Faiz kept crying, Lin and Phillip argued about something, and the yokai continued to stare, whispering to themselves. I could hear them now, pieces of conversation that didn't quite slot together, spoken in dialects older than the house itself and bursts of cutting-edge slang. Here and there, English as punctuation, barely intelligible. Almost none of it made any sense except for the words *bride* and *hello* and *wet*, repeated so many times they soon began to resemble a heartbeat.

hello hello hello

I drank more of the brackish water. This time, the house didn't try to choke me with weeds.

The headache began to ebb, a hum now, like bees had taken residence in the fibrous, grey crenellations of my brain. At least half the lanterns had gone out, and I was thankful for the dimness. I stood and staggered towards Lin and Phillip, the former holding a pose like a demented Peter Pan, fists propped against slim hips.

"Clearly, we need to leave," Lin said.

Phillip shook his head, his lion's mane of blond hair sticky with sweat. "Talia."

"I don't care."

"You don't, but I do." Phillip, for all of his easy swagger, knew the trick of standing smaller, being shorter. Most days, you couldn't tell he was six feet three, an artist's rendition of the American dream. Broad shoulders, muscled thighs, a ruggedly Neolithic jaw. But now he'd given that up, exchanged his approachability for something more contentious, a predatory stillness that drove a scream through the medulla oblongata.

I thought of domestic cats and their wilder cousins, shoulders low to the soil, every paw fitted into the footprint abandoned by the last. I tried not to look down as the smell of ammonia rose sharply, to see whose crotch bloomed with dark stains. It felt rude, somehow. Even indecent. Like I was crossing a line, unmaking one final propriety.

"Yeah, that's you. Go ahead and stay, I guess. But this is when the murders start. You know this is when the murders start." Lin's voice cracked twice through the sentence. He removed his glasses, wiped them along the hem of his shirt. "We're going to die here."

He shuddered. Palmed his face and sang under his breath, giggling as he rocked along his heels.

"Gonna die, gonna die, gonna die. La, la, la. We're all going to die. Because the dead are lonely in the dark, and they all miss the sun."

"Shut. Up." Phillip squeezed the bridge of his nose until the skin beneath blotched. "Shut the fuck up. Shut up, or I'm going to—"

"You're not going to do anything. Lin isn't wrong." What I'd wanted to say was we shouldn't have come here, that there was no reason to stay. I thought of Talia and her sighs, one for every season, the drop of a paisley summer dress along the back of her knees, the breeze in her dark hair, how the dead would suckle the memories from her marrow and be warm for a moment on that. I thought—

I strangled the idea in a fist, took a long breath. "And if you two start fighting, who the fuck is going to do the rescuing? Isn't that your job? You're the all-star quarterback, aren't you? The hero? You're supposed to—"

"Die," Lin whispered.

But Phillip seemed mesmerized, and he gazed at me, mouth slack. I thought of new corpses lying quietly in shallow pools, still lukewarm to the touch, eyes and mouth open as though wedged open with wonder. But slowly, Phillip's tepid stare came alive as I continued to murmur, Scheherazade-like, about everything and nothing, the yokai settling into odalisque poses, an eye-watering collage.

"I guess—no, you're right. We have to—"

"There's a library." Faiz surprised us all with his voice,

his proximity. His eyes burned, their heat an infection. And he kept licking at his upper lip, broad and inquisitive strokes of the tongue, the muscle inflamed, red and swollen with veins. "There's got to be information there."

"Faiz, no," I began.

He sniffed. In the lantern light, his face was more pink than red, more muscle and clotting fluids than skin. Despite the crosshatching of injuries, Faiz seemed docile, almost. "There's a book. There has to be a book. There's always a book—"

"Christ, dude. Your face," said Lin.

"There's a book," said Faiz again. "I know there's a book."

"Dude, that's just fiction. In real life, people don't just leave around solutions like, like it's some kind of video game," I said. "We have to go. I'm sorry. I'm sorry about Talia, but we're going to need to leave. It's too late. We should go. We should go. We need to go. You need help."

"Talia would have stayed for you," Faiz intoned.

No. No, she wouldn't have, I thought. But I couldn't say it, not with the life hollowed out of Faiz's face, pupils pulled to pinholes. His voice was a monotone. "I—"

"You and Lin can go," Phillip said, generous to a sin. "We'll stay."

"Okay," said Lin.

"No." Faiz's hand shot out, rattlesnake-quick, to trap the smaller man's wrist in his grip. Pain spasmed across Lin's face. I could hear the crunch of ligament as his palm folded into itself, thumb pushed so far inland that a muscle juddered in Lin's forearm. But it didn't look like Faiz was out to injure; his expression stayed dreamy, almost drunk. He squeezed and Lin made a noise low in his ribs. "We have to do this together."

"Let go," Lin growled.

Phillip, refereeing: "Be reasonable. If they want to leave—"

Faiz shook his head. The hairs on the nape of my neck tufted. Nausea welled as he turned his attention to Phillip and me, head drooping at an angle. His eyes—

Read a hundred books on horror, and you'll find that every last one possesses at least one mention of someone's eyes gone strange, unfocused and unsettling to witness. I'd always thought it sounded kitschy, hammy, a lazy trope implanted into the creative subconscious by sub-par mentors, pure Hollywood dross. But the look tenanting Faiz's eyes remedied those preconceptions. All the lights were on, and all the ghosts were home too. It wasn't the face of a killer, or the face of a suicide, but someone too exhausted to be either, which was somehow all the worse. When you're tired enough, you'll do anything for sleep.

"We have to do the ritual," Faiz said, no variation in intonation.

"What?"

"The hitobashira ritual. We have to do it. It'd give Talia back. I know it."

Lin's voice spiked. "We're not burying someone to get your fucking girlfriend back."

"I'll be the sacrifice. She's my fiancée. I'll . . . I'll be the one to do it." Faiz somnambulated through phrases: enunciation gone, the crispness of his voice diluted by misery.

"We're not burying you," I said. "We're not going to bury you alive. That's just not happening."

"He's crazy," Lin whispered, expression inscrutable. The space between his thin brows creased. "Plum-stirring mad, although I suppose anyone who was forced to stir plums for hours would go mad. Is that how the line goes? Plum-stirring mad? Plum mad? I don't know. It's such a weird whatchamacallit, don't you—ow."

"Faiz," I said. "Dude, I know what you're thinking. I know you're scared for Talia. I understand it hurts. I understand."

Every hurt I'd ever experienced, every pain accreted from a twenty-four-year pileup of rib-rupturing mistakes distilled into stilted sentences, a look on my face that I hoped said exactly what I needed to say. Faiz stared, the pink tip of his tongue held between his teeth, and slowly, his expression drained to agony.

"You don't understand any of this." He spat, choppily, nearly in tears again, the pitch of his voice going stratospheric towards the end. The yokai applauded. Of course, they'd love it. "You've never had a proper relationship. You don't know what it's like to need someone, to love someone, to—to give a shit. You don't know because you're always too busy running away to whatever new fucking thing you have waiting. You don't understand. You never—"

"Okay, that's enough." Phillip, trying to run interference again, but there wasn't a need. Faiz fell to his knees, Lin's arm finally surrendered, and banged his fists against his ears, crying freely, the sound a scream chaptered into sobs. Phillip followed him down to the tatami, which was no longer pure, no longer clean, rot spiraling through the straw as Lin rubbed at his wrist, the long pale column of his arm boxed in finger marks.

Noting my attention, Lin flicked his gaze up, wrote a circle in the air with a trembling finger, mouthed the word *crazy*. I couldn't tell who he meant. Faiz or him or me or the entirety of our codependent coven, our audience besides, the blind damning the blind, a theatre of dead fools. I swallowed vomit, thin as gruel and warm.

My vision had ceased to gyre but it wouldn't stop bobbing, and I felt like I'd been anchored to the bottom of a pond, looking up through a mirror of green water. I thought of girls nibbled by fish and freshwater prawns, their ribs like combs, how long it'd take for a corpse to be whittled to bone by such a harmless menagerie. I thought of death again, and unclean things stirring in the mud.

"Do we even know there's a book there?" I heard myself say.

"Of course there is. We saw them when we got in. This place, this place is rotten with books. There were libraries everywhere. We're going to have answers there. I know."

"Jesus." Lin stared out the door. I followed his gaze to where blind eyes, bulbous and luminous as fresh grapes, clustered in the gap. They blinked, skin frothing up from inside the mass, and, for a moment, they became scrotal-like. "Jesus, it's the whole fucking house, Cat."

"They don't need to stay if they don't want to," said Phillip.

I dampened my lips, licked the sour from the cracked flesh. "People die when they split up. We gotta stay together. Besides, it can't be that far away—"

"Next room."

"See?" A smile twitched feebly. "Not far away."

"Did you just literally say we should stay? Cat." Lin's voice, coming up from behind me, nails shoveling into my collarbone. "What the fuck? What the fuck are you doing?"

I whirled on him, all teeth. "We're not splitting up."

"Fuck."

"Jesus, you fucking pieces of—" Phillip roared into the clamor, shutting us all up. "Just—just fucking stop. I'm so sick of you fucking idiots. Single file. Let's just fucking get to the library. If there's no book, you two leave. We'll go on ahead."

"Always the hero, aren't you?" Lin giggled, but no one'd look at him twice, not that he cared, content with his lunacy. Through all of it, Faiz said nothing, watched the door like his true love stood in the slit, bubbling with eyes, so many of them now, bubbles spilling from the mouth of a Coke bottle. "Bet Faiz loves it. Bet Faiz loves the idea you'd be the one who has his back. Bet it'd turn out great for you."

"Shut up, Lin," I said.

"We're going to regret this."

I ignored him. "Let's go."

CHAPTER 7

t wasn't so much a library as much as it was an archive of corpses, manuscripts chewed up by the centuries, edges winnowed by insects. Their leather festered with mold, with mushrooms, wide-brimmed with fluting bodies, tiered like cheap apartments and blanched by the half-light. Some could barely be labeled as books anymore, their paper digested then regurgitated as building material. There were so many of them. Wasp nests, almost intestinal in look, built atop the remains of a termitarium, its inhabitants long dead. Suddenly, I was reminded of dried alveoli, pressed and preserved between glass, something an old girlfriend had shown off between kisses in the classroom.

"There's a book here."

"Yes," I said, voice hoarse. I thought the same things that Lin and Phillip must have been thinking, the two exchanging uncertain expressions, Lin's madness receded to a jouncing energy, Phillip's face closed up like a casket as he set candles through the room. There was certainly a book here. There were countless books here, adrift in dead insects and wriggling ivory larvae.

The yokai had followed us, a conga line of myths, repeating between themselves hello. Hello. Hello. Like infants or parrots, or maybe something fresh-born and wetly glistening, amazed to have larynx and lips, the zygote of a vocabulary. Hello, the kitsune sang to each other. Hello, said the kappa, the red-faced oni, the gashadokuro, bent low and crawling on its knuckles. Hello.

"I—" Faiz fluttered his hands before sweeping a stack of mouldering books into the cradle of an arm. "Why are you all just standing around? Let's look."

Phillip plunged into the labour, both hands, no doubts at all, and dug into the refuse like a dog, his mouth chewing through prayers or curses, I couldn't tell which. Couldn't tell if it mattered, not with the fever of his articulation. Lin and I exchanged a look, anxious.

"This is bullshit." Lin put to the voice what we'd both been thinking, but we all knew there wouldn't be follow-through. The only way out was through a door teeming with yokai, their fingers clenched all around the doorway. Hello, they whispered. Hello, hello. "There is no way we're going to find anything in here. There's no way there's anything to find. This is a fool's errand. And how the fuck are you even sure that Talia—"

"Ah-hah!"

Lin startled, stumbled back. Faiz staggered to us in a kind of bowlegged trot, no bend to his joints, no cadence. His palm bookmarked a massive ledger, the vellum spidered with black characters. He slapped the page, once, twice, four times, arrhythmic yet with intent, like he was freestyling a new argot of Morse code. Jabbed a finger at the crosshatching of lines, face shining with triumph.

"Everything we need," he said.

I flicked a look down. The lines regarded me in return: ink-stroke eyes between the characters, mouths in the logograms. I swallowed. "Faiz."

"It says—" He tapped the opened page. Silverfish writhed across the paper over and around and between the web of his fingers, antennae slick with light. The iconography on the pages made no sense, black scratches imposed by an alien hand. They bloomed beneath Faiz's fingers and the pages went black, and through the glass of the ink, something grinned. "That this place is consecrated to the Four Kings, and each of them requires a different sacrifice."

CASSANDRA KHAW

"There's nothing on the fucking page," Phillip said, quiet, in that way he did when he was genuinely angry, a hum in the backbeat of his voice. "It's just mould."

"A bit of blood, a bit of bone, a bit of cum," Faiz retorted, his cheeks blotching red. "A bit of organ. Four cardinal directions. Four Kings. That's what it says. Cat?"

"I'm staying out of this."

I gave Phillip a look, hoping he'd get what I was trying to telegraph: let him have this. Maybe we might get lucky. Maybe all the yokai wanted was for us to panic, kick around a few old books, cry, then they'd let us out with Talia a little worse for wear. Either way, I wasn't going to correct Faiz. Not now with the Sword of Damocles metronoming over our heads, shaving the moments into halves, into quarters, into an infinitely replicating prism of drawn-out pauses, underscored with a war chant of: this was a fucking mistake. If Faiz was right, if the myths were true, Talia lay buried with every dead girl to have been entombed in this place. How many minutes and how many hours before she suffocated on soil?

Phillip laved his tongue over his mouth, licking the sweat from his upper lip, and tried to smile even though it made him look like a goldfish drowning on dry air.

I grimaced and tried not to stare at the walls.

"A bit of organ." Faiz had aged sixty years in six hours. Not literally. Although you'd think he had, if all you saw were his mirror image in the fusuma. The house had made a twin of Faiz in its walls, aged that calligraphed version of him into some kind of hairless Chow Chow, thick-faced and jowly, sad eyes down-turned in a face wadded like dough. Who knew that dead feudal lords could be so petty? "I'll do it."

"What?" I shot my head up.

"I'll do it," he repeated, even as his gold-leafed dop-pelgänger creased and crinkled, the paper ripping into a train of mouths. I could smell out-of-season zelkova and frangipani, spider lilies the color of arteries, incense and grave dirt, the odour so thick you could knot it into a noose. "Life doesn't have any meaning without her, anyway. I can't—I don't want to go on in a world without her. I'll do it. I'll cut out my heart. I'll—"

I slapped him. "What the fuck?"

It was a good slap. More of an open-palm hook, his jaw crunching where the joint met the heel of my hand. The blow rattled through both of us so hard that it made me bite my tongue. Blood dripped warm down the eave of my scowl, dotting the now-rotten tatami with red. A breeze billowed past us, a stench too: cardamom and mildew and menstrual flow. Around us, the yokai in the murals jeered and snickered in Chaplinesque quiet: ink-stroke tanuki and painted tengu, kitsune drawn with six strokes of a master's brush, a two-dimensional heron gorgeted in carnelian, the color so bright you'd think someone had slit its throat.

"You're not cutting your fucking heart out. What the fucking fuck do you think this is? A fucking Shakespeare tragedy or some fucking shit like this? We're not fucking letting you—"

Faiz never got angry. Except when he did. He roared up like a bear, like someone who'd run out of reasons to keep breathing, fists balled around the loss of his bride-to-be, his almost-wife. I squared my feet and jutted my chin. Faiz was tall when he wasn't slouched over, six feet even on the rise of his toes, quarterback shoulders. He could have been a somebody but all he ever wanted to be was somebody to someone, a husband, a family man, a dream he'd coddled since he was ten.

"The fuck do you think you're doing?"

"The fuck do you think *you're* doing?" Like hell I was going to stand down for an ego swollen as an alcoholic's liver, bruised black, bleeding warm pus and grief. Mourning's got a way of making men out of mice, I tell you. I shoved him and he leaned hard into the push, one arm brought up over his head.

"Whoa, guys—" Wonderboy Phillip, glossy as the cover of *Forbes,* hundred-dollar clean fade and a jawline to slice open your heart, slid between us. You could always count on Phillip to save the day. Forget the initial argument. He had room to play hero.

"Fuck off." I stomped a heel into his calf, a thumb's length south of the back of his knee, snarling as I spun away. Phillip slung me a wounded-dog look, the candle-glow picking out the gold in his hair. In the next room, a perfect black silhouette on white rice paper, kane-mizu on ivory, the ohaguro-bettari sat and laughed like someone'd told her the joke that killed God.

CHAPTER 8

D on't touch me," said Faiz.

"Jesus. We're all friends here, man." Phillip held his palms up, guiltless as a madonna, features twitching through the permutations of a smile. He had lost the trick of the expression, somehow, somewhere between arrival and the time that Faiz wrenched out his own tooth, a strand of red nerve whipping through the half-gold light.

We could be dead.

You'd think it'd be harder. But if you're desperate enough, you can shovel under the gum with your nails, digging out sickle-moons of bleeding pink flesh until the bicuspid loosens, pre-slickened with blood, and you can anchor a grip around the root and pull. At least we'd kept him from cutting out his heart. At least there was that. Faiz had fucked his own hand raw, trying to eke out a little bit of spunk to drip into the floorboards. But it could have been worse.

"If you were my friend, you'd let me die—"

He pushed and Phillip did not yield, a summer romance with the runway separating the two, Phillip's post-collegiate musculature longer, leaner, still built to be loved by the light. Next to the other man, Faiz looked old, tired, middle-aged before his season. "Are you listening to yourself? Do you have any idea how melodramatic you sound?"

I sat down as the two continued to bicker, chest to calisthenics-honed chest, shoulders scissored back, like one of them was on the precipice of inviting the other to waltz. On the walls, the yokai danced like they invented the idea, pirouetting through genres and periods, Nara to Muromachi, every shogunate of literati painting, austere to aureate, twelve bodies to a cosmic tango.

"You okay?" Lin touched fingers to my shoulder.

I looked up into his narrow face, kabuki pale, shaped like some kumadori artist had taken a brush to his bones, all slant and sharpness. A fox's countenance, too clever even behind Coke-bottle glasses. The ohaguro-bettari stood behind his shoulder, smiling, every tooth capped in ink, so close to his cheek that he had to feel her breath on his ear. A stench of vinegar and rust seeped everywhere, and I tried not to think about silk and white satin, so many yards of both, enough to bury a corpse six times over. "No. There is no fucking way I could be okay."

"Tell me about it." Lin smiled like he meant it. We both knew he didn't. He lit a cigarette—hand-rolled, cut with tamarind peel and weed—and squatted beside me, smoke curling between his teeth. The ohaguro-bettari followed, kneeling beside him, beside us. Lin didn't look at her once.

But I did. I stared at the yokai as I took a toke from Lin's joint. She had the angles of someone carefully starved from cradle to nuptials, clavicle and collarbone in stark chiaroscuro. Her skin didn't just look like porcelain, it *was* porcelain, enameled and gleaming, faultless save for her red mouth; no eyes, no nose, no philtrum, not even the conceit of cheekbones. But even her flesh wasn't as pale as the shiromuku she wore, the satin the color of expensive chalk.

"We could just go, you know?"

"No."

"The doors aren't locked. The manor isn't keeping us in here."

"Is that so?"

"Cat." He plucked the cigarette from my fingers, his voice gentle as he could make it, the same timbre as the one you'd extend to a suicide risk: slightly frightened, too much syncopation. Lin's breath plumed white. It'd gotten cold again in the last few minutes. "He isn't your responsibility."

I exhaled on my fingertips, the nails already purpling at the base. "He's my best friend."

"And an absolute fucking idiot." A bristling of rage—not anger, Lin never did anything halfway—like the pelt of a dog rubbed the wrong way, his smile vicious.

I nodded. There wasn't much else to say so we sat for a long minute, passing the cigarette between us until it shriveled to an ember, Faiz and Phillip fighting the whole while. They'd diversified to character attacks, petty insults, all those years of friendship run through the abattoir, back and forth until every secret was turned inside out. Any second now, something was going to snap, a neck or a temper or a spine.

I looked over. The ohaguro-bettari was smiling like an ingénue at her first soiree, a blood-soaked husband on the horizon. He'd be the last man to stagger from the killing block, an axe in his hands, and that's how you knew he was the one. Because he was a survivor, Mr. Take No Prisoner.

"Look, I'm not going to insult your intelligence. We both know exactly what's going to happen next. One of them"—Lin jerked his chin at the pair, his fingers curling with mine and when he squeezed, I squeezed back, hard as I could, like our hands could keep us moored in normal—"is going to say something really fucking stupid. The other one is going to snap. If it's Faiz, he'll get a boost of adrenaline and he's going to grab Phillip, and they're both going to wrestle until Faiz somehow manages to accidentally impale him on a piece of scenery."

"And if it's Phillip?"

Lin had a laugh like a bark, like a wound weeping sepsis. "Faiz is going to die outright. Duh."

⊸≺∗≻⊸

This is the problem with horror movies:

Everyone knows what's coming next but actions have momentum, every decision an equal and justified reaction. Just because you know you should, doesn't mean that you can, stop.

⊸≺∗≻⊸

Phillip moved first.

If I was a betting woman, I'd have put money on Faiz being the one to break the stalemate. I'd have gambled on his idiocy. Grief makes us worse people. But it was Phillip who pulled the metaphorical trigger, knuckles gore-smeared as he drew his knuckles back from Faiz's face, vermillion and black. Faiz gawped at him, palm cupped beneath his jaw, nose bridge split in three spaces, the tip concave. He drooled blood and rills of mucus.

"You broke my nose." *You brok muh nus.* Enunciation is a bastard when your nasal septum has been flattened, and your mouth is sticky with salt and snot. Faiz swallowed, rubbed his thumb along his chin. The skin stayed red and wet.

"I—" Phillip shook out his fist and stared at Faiz, stupefied. Golden-boy Phillip, good-guy Phillip, valedictorian, voted "Most Likely to Succeed" seven consecutive years in a row, cut down at the knees, no more exceptional than your average punk, another man's blood curdling between his fingers. He wiped his hand over his face, leaving four lines across his cheeks. "I didn't mean to."

His voice was a hush, full of shame for the sin he'd committed against better judgment. Men like Phillip don't punch people. Except when they do.

"You broke my fucking nose."

"It was an accident—"

"You fucking punched me."

"Dude. I'm sorry. I didn't mean to hit you. You were

just going off the rails there—I. I didn't know what else to do. It was an accident, okay? I wasn't thinking." He breathed out. "I wasn't thinking."

Beside me, Lin was unfolding, uncurling to his full height, slim as my waning hopes. Ohaguro-bettari. Nothing but blackened teeth. Nothing but teeth stained with tannic acids and ferric compounds. An old girl-friend told me once about the unguent that the aristo-crats used: iron fillings fermented in vinegar, in tea, in cups of sake, stirred with gallnuts from the sumac tree until it became something that'd stick.

I wondered for a second what the mixture would taste like, if it'd be like kissing copper from the ohaguro's tongue, if I could content myself knowing the last per-son I kiss was a dead woman's ghost.

"This is the part where we all die," Lin whispered.

Faiz pulled a knife. Of course he did. There was no timeline where he wouldn't have escalated, wouldn't have found a knife or a gun or a jag of glass. Something heavy enough to breach the skull, pulp the brain into paste. He swung as I staggered to my feet, a scream loaded in my lungs. No artistry to the swoop of his arm but a knife is a knife is a knife is a sharp edge meant to split the seams of the skin, open up the torso and let in the light.

I bayed like a wolf under the lunatic moon as blood

gushed free. Muscles relaxed and gravity tugged; slick reams of purple-grey intestine unspooled from the gash in Phillip's belly. Faiz had cut so deep. Lin grabbed me, both arms. I howled. Phillip spasmed onto the tatami, every convulsion disgorging another palmful of viscera, clawing at his entrails but they wouldn't fit back inside.

The room smelled of gastric juices and vomit, of urine and bowels. The room smelled of blood. The room smelled of the man my best friend had murdered. The room smelled of dying.

"Help me." His face was whiter than paint.

"Don't," Lin hissed into my ear. I couldn't tell what he meant, if what he was saying was don't engage, or don't try because we are in act three and barreling down to the end, or don't look. Don't let this be the thing you remember about Phillip, golden boy, dead boy, organs slopping out of his side.

I didn't cry.

Don't let anyone tell you I did. People expect certain weaknesses from girls. But they don't cry over a man they'd never loved, could not love, even if he said he respected the swagger of her insouciance, her post-punk rhetoric, even though he said maybe and she said she couldn't. I didn't cry for Phillip.

I didn't cry for any of them.

I didn't.

I swear.

CHAPTER 9

O h, god." The words clattered out of Faiz. "Oh, god. Oh, god. Oh, god. Oh, god."

He repeated them until they hitched in his throat, always snagging on the second syllable, until all it sounded like was Faiz saying *oh* and *oh* again, quieter each time. He sagged to his knees. The knife slid from his fingers.

"I didn't mean to. I'm sorry. I'm sorry. I'm sorry."

Phillip moaned. The sound could have meant anything.

"Don't," Lin told me again, his mouth in my hair. I could feel his jaw mold the consonants, the motions of his lips. "There's no point. We can't stop the bleeding. We're five hundred miles away from the nearest hospital. I don't have anything—" His voice tore. "He's

‣ 115 ‣

going to die, Cat. He's dead. He's dead. So, don't look. Don't."

I did anyway. I shrugged his embrace apart and shambled towards where Phillip lay, bile and blood soaking into the mouldering straw. I read somewhere that it takes about twenty minutes to die from disembowelment, which doesn't sound long at all but hurt has a way of stretching out a heartbeat into an infinity of going colder, slower, every breath another starburst of too much to cope with, lighting up the cerebrum with constellations of anguish. Phillip's eyes were rolled up to the whites and he stank of piss. I didn't know someone else's pain could have a texture, a bite, a gelatinousness you could hold in your teeth, but I could almost gnaw on Phillip's dying.

"Cat." Faiz knuckled at his own eyes, crying without embarrassment, his face a slaughterhouse of bruises and reds. "I didn't mean to. I didn't mean—you know I wouldn't hurt anyone. It was an accident. I didn't mean to. I didn't. I'm sorry. I'm sorry."

The ohaguro-bettari laughed. The sound was a knife, was a hole like an eye opening beneath the ribs, was the memory of one man being held up to the shining light of another, one man being less than, second-best, always inferior to the other. The sound was a thought: wouldn't it make all the sense in the world to let that lack of self-worth move your hand, just a little, just for a second while no one's watching?

"You're sorry," I repeated. I wanted to touch Phillip, let my fingers drag through his hair, the pale strands clumped to his cheek like letters and when I scrunched my eyes a certain way, they almost read like *liar*.

"Sure you are." Lin's voice shook. "Sure. Abso-fucking-lutely. You have absolutely no motivation at all to kill the guy your fiancée used to date. The Greek god to your sedentary geek. No reason. Nothing like that ever crossed your consciousness. In fact, you're so sure about this being an accident, you can guarantee this never crossed your subconscious either."

"Are you saying I murdered him?" There was no threat in his voice, only incredulity, shame in the slurry of his speech.

"I did not. The words 'Faiz murdered Phillip' never crossed my lips. Nope. No, sir. Or any variations of the statement. Ask Cat. She's right here. She'd tell you if—"

"Lin. Stop it." The ohaguro-bettari had moved again, blurring from where she'd sat behind us to kneeling at Phillip's head, his skull pillowed on her lap. She crooned to him with a mockingbird's warble. His breathing slackened. "You're not helping the situa—"

"What situation?" Lin grinned wider, half-screaming, arms flung out. He spun like a top and the yokai twirled with him, expressions ecstatic. "There's no situation here. Faiz absolutely did not take advantage of a situation to murder Phillip. No one would dare dream about saying anything like that. Not with the knife still in reach."

"Lin!"

"I'm sorry. I'm sorry." *M'awwy. M'awwy.* Faiz burrowed his face into his palms.

My lungs felt full. Heaving with earth, and wet concrete, and fingertips grated down to the bone. I swallowed and snarled: "The book—does anyone remember what the fuck the book said?"

Both men shut up.

"I—" I ran a hand through my hair, swallowed, swallowed again, but the reek of Phillip's insides persisted, a sour caul gloving my tongue, the back of my mouth tasting muddily of coins. *You know there was nothing in that book*, a voice in my head reminded me. But we're past that. This is past logic. "You said it was a bit of blood, a bit of cum, a bit of bone, and a bit of organ." I swallowed a third time, ran my tongue over my teeth. "Do either of you remember if it was meant to be fresh?"

"No, no, no. Cat," Lin hissed. "What the fuck?"

"Probably fresh, I guess," I continued, six thousand miles away, numb in a way that made me wonder if I'd ever come home to myself, every word another lock to keep me out. "That'd make the most sense. That's why it is human sacrifice and not grave digging."

Faiz stared at me like I'd told him the secret names of the prophets, the private and the profane, the sacred alphabet shared by devotee and deity. He looked at me like I'd taken up the memory of his first word and given him a corpse instead. "I didn't mean to."

"I know," I said, all the while thinking *you're lying, you're lying, you're lying.* A decade of friendship teaches you a lot of things: the tics that separate *I'm sorry* and *I'm sorry you caught me,* that hangdog expression that is really code for when the other person's expecting you to fix their mess.

I wondered what they saw in my face.

I leaned down and warmed my hand in Phillip's belly. He shuddered at the contact.

"I know," I said again, tired, the lie practically lit up in red neon lights. "I know. But Phillip's dying, so we— I—let's make it count for something, I guess."

⸺›❈‹⸺

We dug a hole at the base of the fourth pillar and placed Phillip's viscera into that cradle of shallow loam, one coil at a time. Faiz and Lin fought over whether we should cut his throat or whether we should measure out his offal and fill another three holes, just to be sure. One last act of mercy for the man we'd known since we were all sixteen, or have his death matter. But then the manor sighed—a long, slow breath, a dying man's breath spun of silk filaments—and suddenly, there was Talia, propped up against a wall, still garlanded in her wedding whites.

It was exactly like the fairy tales promised: a little blood, a little bone, a little cum, a little bit of organ, and the manor returned the girl of Faiz's dreams. She smelled of the earth and summer sunlight. Honeysuckle and fabric softener and skin warmed on a stoop in the sun. When Faiz took Talia in his arms, Phillip's heart gave out, one last exhausted pump. He died alone while our backs were turned. Twenty-four years of being the center of everyone's attention and that's how he went out, not with a bang or a whimper, just a sigh and the world going colder and the last light from the lanterns dimming to nothing, fireflies in blind eyes.

We went home after that.

What else were we supposed to do?

EPILOGUE

When Phillip's parents called to tell us there'd be a memorial in Vermont, that ancestral home his mother would say a hundred times she'd regretted leaving, none of us made excuses. We showed up in our funerary best: me in a black dress, Lin in his long coat, and Faiz in a suit that no longer fit. Talia stayed in the hospital, nursing her nightmares.

There were policemen at the wake but they stood loose-stanced and long-bodied, bored already of their assignment. No awkward sympathy mottled their paired expressions. They slouched in a corner, hunkered over YouTube videos, only occasionally subjecting the crowd to halfhearted audits. I didn't blame them. Compassion, like everything else, can be worn dull by rough use.

Moreover, the investigation was closed. Before we came home, we'd turned the mansion into Phillip's pyre. Then we lied on repeat until the fiction became as natural as terror: *there was alcohol, there was a fire, there was a panic.* When we came out, we realized we were one short. By then, it was too late.

It worked.

Somehow, they believed us.

Phillip's death was a mistake, said the doctors and the detectives, the reporters and the neighbours until, one by one, drained of conspiracies and condolences, they went away. At Lin's behest, we skewered Phillip on a jut of broken timber, let what remained of him unravel, spread like Christmas lights. Lit a fire. Watched it burn.

There was nothing to find.

There was nothing found.

And all at once, it was over.

Phillip stopped being Phillip.

He became instead a closed casket and terse conversations, a house with every curtain drawn shut. Phillip's mother wafted between her guests like a spectre, her beauty-queen face veiled, her hands gloved in velvet.

"I'm sorry," I said to her.

Phillip's mother, gorgeous even in despair, sobbed into my shoulder, while I prayed that her son's ghost might find its way home. He had been his parents' only son. Their sweet heir, their shining light, their hope.

"I'm sorry," I said again. I didn't have breath for anything else.

His mother gave us three pairs of cufflinks, pretty as you please, identical wolf heads with dewdrops of opals for eyes. Because Phillip thought of us as his pack, she said. She gave me a box I recognized from Phillip's nineteenth birthday. I'd put his shirt inside, the one he left behind in my dorm room. In it, she'd stacked his comic books: the mint-condition, first-edition ones he always said he'd give me. *Insurance against a bad year,* Phillip had insisted that winter's morning, as we lay there under the sunroof, not together but not anything like friends. *I could pawn them for all the Subway sandwiches I wanted,* he said, and smiled like the sun came out for him alone.

"If you remember anything else. Anything else at all," she said, pressing the box into my grip. "Tell us. We won't blame you. We know bad things happen."

We said nothing. After everything that had happened, how could we? We tucked the lie of Phillip's death between Starbucks pick-me-ups and takeout dinners, Skype conversations and police interrogations, kept repeating its specifics until we almost believed it. Then, we tucked ourselves into our own lives, drifting until we were nothing but Facebook notifications to each other, an endless circuit of birthdays and likes and curated photographs.

I went back to school. Six months before, you couldn't have put the idea in front of me without making me laugh. But after everything that had happened, I decided I needed a do-over. So, I went back to school. Oxford University, to be exact. Economics, with a minor in accounting. Neat numbers. Tidy things, unlike what happened so many months ago.

Lately, I've begun to wonder if the ohaguro-bettari followed us from the manor. I see her, sometimes. Or at least, I think I do. Reflected in the windows, her face as wan as mine. But it is always my reflection, the eyes smudged of definition, the mouth blotted in shadow so it looks like there's nothing but blackened teeth.

ACKNOWLEDGMENTS

Thanks to Ellen Datlow, first and foremost, for believing in this book when I couldn't make heads or tails of its worth. It literally wouldn't exist if not for you going, "I like this, but it needs a lot of work."

To the team at Nightfire for this and everything else, and especially Kristin Temple for helping me survive bureaucracy.

To Michael Curry for being my long-suffering agent and indomitable supporter.

To Richard Kadrey, Ali Trota, Olivia Wood, Linda Nguyen, Shoma Patnaik, Gary Astleford, Chris Blake, and Brian Kindregan, I adore all of you. Thank you for being there throughout a rough year.